Svetlana Simonov of the government's top-secret Omega Force is sent from Washington D.C. to Kiev, Ukraine, to assassinate an international drug dealer, Boris Antonich, to put his organization out of business and give him the death sentence he so richly deserves. Unbeknownst to her, that is *exactly* the same assignment that Dmitri Kuzetsov, top assassin for Russia's infamous intelligence agency, the GRU, has been given. Svetlana and Dmitri — natural deadly enemies — must become the unlikeliest of allies in their shared assignment. Svetlana and Dmitri soon find themselves working side by side in their international search for the cunning and elusive drug kingpin. During the hunt for their prey, these two secret agents find their unquenchable passion for each other runs red-hot as savage violence and non-stop action grips them every step of the way.

Too Many Assassins
Copyright © 2020 Robin Gideon
ISBN: 978-1-4874-2960-7
Cover art by Martine Jardin

Published by eXtasy Books Inc or
Devine Destinies, an imprint of eXtasy Books Inc

Look for us online at:
www.eXtasybooks.com or www.devinedestinies.com

Too Many Assassins
Agent (Rom)antics Book 3

By

Robin Gideon

DEDICATION

This one is for Jay, Nicki, Brigit, and Cat.
And, of course, for Keith.

CHAPTER ONE

Washington D.C., United States

Jefferson Burke, one of the senior administrative operatives working for America's top-secret espionage agency, Omega Force, sat in an overstuffed easy chair in a luxury hotel in Washington D.C., and wondered what Svetlana Simonov would be wearing. Sometimes she was strictly professional, wearing the clothes of a thousand dollar-an-hour attorney working for a firm that did a lot of business with the U.S. government, and no one else. At other times she dressed like a not-yet-thirty socialite who liked to show off the fact that she had beautiful breasts and legs, and that she knew both men and women liked to see them. Sometimes her skirts modesty came down to the tops of her knees. Sometimes her miniskirts and mini dresses barely came to the tops of her thighs. The pretty panties that she wore would most definitely be seen by anyone interested in finding out about such things. Burke had no doubt that many people were interested.

Burke would find out about her lingerie soon. He always did.

Looking at his wristwatch, Burke saw that it was two minutes to three. He had said he wanted to see her at three, and since he demanded punctuality from Svetlana, she was always on time. Not just to the minute, but to the second. If she was the tiniest bit late, he punished her for the transgression. Administering punishment to Svetlana was one of the great turn-ons of Burke's life.

1

Burke punished his field agent often, and he always tried to think of a new way of delivering his wrath. He didn't want to fall into the trap of expected outcomes. Svetlana deserved so much more than that.

There was a faint rap of knuckles on the door of his hotel room. Before rising from his chair, he looked at his wrist-watch. It was precisely three o'clock. She was *exactly* on time, so he'd have to figure out another reason to punish her. This wouldn't be a problem. There were countless reasons. His only question was picking the right one.

He rose from his chair and crossed the room. He opened the door without first asking who was there or looking through the small spyglass. It could only be one person, and that person happened to be the most beautiful, talented, sensual woman he had ever encountered in his life. She was also a shockingly effective field agent for Omega Force.

He opened the door and, as always, the first sight of Svetlana Simonov caused the breath to catch in his chest and his heartrate to accelerate. The urge to take her immediately into his arms and kiss her was so strong it required an act of will-power for him to restrain himself. Rather than act on impulse, he let his gaze slide slowly from the top of her head down to the toes of her high-heeled stilettos.

Barefoot, she stood five-foot-nine. In the red-soled stilettos, she was six-foot-two, and every inch of her was impressive.

Her hair was streaked honey blonde and fell down in waves well over her shoulders. She had a fine forehead, and beneath it, a medium nose that was neither large nor small. It was her eyes, though, that one noticed instantly and remembered forever. They were the color of blue water, but whether it was icy cold Anchorage water or bath-water warm Key West water was debatable. What wasn't up for debate was whether or not her eyes were stunningly beautiful. They were, and everyone—both men and women—agreed on this indisputable fact. With one's gaze moving southward, there were shoulders which were proportionate to her body, and then her breasts, which were full and round and rather more extravagant than most women's bosom. She made no effort to draw attention to them; they did that all by themselves. Her waist narrowed dramatically, and her hips rounded nicely. The thighs suggested at a certain athleticism and were tapered. The calves led to feet which were inevitably caressed by the finest and most famous — and expensive — cobblers in the world.

She was, from toes to hairline and beyond, an immediate cause of favorable sexual response for Jefferson Burke, and for everyone else who had the significant good fortune of looking at her.

For this meeting she had chosen to wear a navy-blue blazer with matching knee-length skirt, a white silk blouse, and rather ostentatious three carat blue-white diamond stud earrings. In contrast, her makeup was subdued, her eye shadow hazy shades of dark and light blue, and administered with the lightest touch.

"Thank you for coming, Agent Simonov," Burke said, his tone crisp and thoroughly military and professional. "Please, come in."

"Thank you, sir," Svetlana replied as she walked past him and into the room.

With nowhere else to sit, she sat on the foot of the bed, which was directly in front of the chair and desk that Burke had been at only moments earlier.

Perfect. Burke drank in the visual beauty of Svetlana sitting on the bed. *Exactly as I had planned.*

His cock was beginning to grow into a formidable, impressively sized erection. It wouldn't bother him in the least if Svetlana noticed the effect her presence and beauty had on him. He walked slowly back to his chair, then sat in it. By the time he crossed his legs, putting his right ankle on his left knee, his cock had reached full extension, and was threatening to burst out of the confines of his immaculately tailored trousers.

He was pleased to see that Svetlana noticed.

She folded her hands in her lap while sitting at the foot of the bed, and questioned rather quietly, "Sir?"

The tone of her voice, in the single, spoken word, made Burke desperately want to ravish her instantly. The blood flowed in his veins like lava.

"I have another assignment for you, and I apologize that it comes so soon after your last one, but things happen in the world and we have to respond accordingly." As she started to respond, he raised his hand to silence her. "Before we speak of the next assignment, I think we should address some issues of the last one. I've just read your post-assignment report, and I find some aspects of it . . . troubling."

He watched when she shivered. He could feel the blood pumping in his veins.

"Your mission was to find Gunther Krueger, discover the identity of his informant, and neutralize both of them, wasn't it?"

Before answering she crossed her legs at the knee, tugged her skirt down slightly, and folded her hands in her lap. She looked into his eyes and said quietly, "Yes, sir."

"And you were successful in that, were you not?"

"Yes, sir. I was successful. Neither man will ever again be selling IED bombmaking technology to terrorists."

"How ironic that you used a bomb to kill them. That was a good weapon-of-choice. The authorities in Lebanon came to the conclusion that they accidentally blew themselves up."

"That was exactly as I had wanted, sir."

"Did you also want to have sex with them?"

He watched as Svetlana inhaled sharply, then held her

breath for a moment. After several silent seconds she said, "No, sir. But it was necessary for the success of the assignment."

"You had sex with Krueger first, and after he introduced you to the informant, you seduced him. A few days later you had sex with them both at the same time, did you not?"

"I had to get the two of them together to dispense justice simultaneously. If I neutralized one of them first, then the other would go underground."

"At least that's the excuse you gave in your report."

"But—"

Svetlana's explanation for her conduct was cut off when Burke gave her an icy glare.

When she cast her gaze down at her folded hands in her lap, Burke allowed himself a slight smile, since she couldn't see it. He felt his pulse pounding in his erection, and it seemed as though every nerve in his body was taut and quivering, like a thoroughbred racehorse at the starting gate.

"Stand up, please." His tone was deceptively casual. When Svetlana stood, the urge to sexually overpower her immediately washed over him like a gigantic Hawaiian ocean wave, terrifying to everyone except the very best of surfers. He rested his hands lightly on the arms of the desk chair. He cleared his throat lightly, then said, "You sucked cock during your assignment, didn't you?" Svetlana didn't answer. Burke waited silently for a few seconds. "You might just as well admit it to me in person. You did, after all, include this information in your report."

"Y-yes, sir," Svetlana said in a whisper, with a slight stammer. "I performed fellatio while on assignment."

"Quite a lot, it seems. You gave them both blow jobs, each of them several times." She nodded, her gaze cast at the tips of her red-soled stilettos. "Did you swallow their cum?" She shook her head. "Oh?" he prompted, his tone suggesting suspicion.

Svetlana lifted her chin, looked Burke in the eyes, and replied, "Sometimes. If I thought that the situation warranted it, and if such action couldn't be avoided."

Burke rose to his feet, taking the few steps it took to be at her side. He towered over her. Burke began loosening his silk necktie.

"The last time you were with them in a *ménage a trois* —"

"That happened only once," Svetlana said quickly, looking up into Burke's eyes. After several seconds, her gaze lowered submissively. "Just that one time, then I left them and detonated the bomb."

"Was it exciting having such dangerous, murderous men fucking your pussy and mouth at the same time?" Burke loosened the knot of the necktie to slip the silk over his head, though he kept it knotted. "You're sure you're telling the truth?"

"Yes, sir."

"You have been known to lie. Now stand up and put your hands behind your back," Burke said with quiet iron-hard authority and more than just a hint of malice. "Cross them at the wrists." She did as she had been commanded as Burke walked slowly around her. He pushed her blouse cuffs up just enough so that the silk necktie surrounded her bare wrists, very near the small gold wristwatch that had diamonds to indicate the hours. He cinched the necktie tightly, and Svetlana uttered a short, soft gasp as her bondage was secured. "That should keep you from causing too much mischief."

He walked around Svetlana once more. When he faced her, he stood so close that he could smell the delicate perfume she had placed on her throat and between her breasts. It was Chanel No. 5, and it suited her perfectly. He was aware that the very best always suited Svetlana perfectly.

"I send you on an assignment, and you always find some

way of getting yourself into trouble." He eased the fingers of his right hand into the silky blonde hair at Svetlana's left ear. He filtered her hair through his fingers as he brushed the strands back so that they hung over her shoulder. Her breasts were rising and falling more rapidly now that he was touching her. Burke liked that response. "Lovely hair." He stroked his fingertips down slowly, then slid the side of his thumb over her slender arched eyebrow. "Lovely eyes. The bluest I've ever seen." He caressed her cheek, and as he did so, he ran his thumb over her lips. "Lovely mouth. Lips made for telling lies . . . and sucking cock."

Svetlana gasped and turned her face aside, and Burke knew that he was running out of time. His lustful impatience was testimony to Svetlana's extravagant allure.

Burke ran his fingertips along Svetlana's throat, then down between the mounds of her breasts. Her nipples made noticeable dents in the fabric of her blouse and bra. He fought against the urge to tear her blouse open, rip off her bra, and then feast upon her breasts. But to do that would be to accelerate the pace of this encounter. It was always more satisfying, he knew, to enjoy intemperate pleasures in a leisurely manner.

Having successfully avoided touching Svetlana's breasts, Burke raised his hand, his fingertips caressing her skin very lightly. He once more caressed her face, then he pushed his fingers into the hair at the top of Svetlana's head. While looking into her round obviously frightened eyes, he clenched his fingers slowly into a fist.

"You're always getting yourself into trouble." He gave her head a quick, harsh shake, pulling on her hair. Svetlana gasped, and her mouth opened. "You know that when you get yourself into trouble, then I have to punish you." Burke began putting downward pressure on Svetlana. She resisted. "On your knees." It was a coldly spoken command, one that

7

Svetlana could not disobey. She sank to her knees in the luxury hotel suite, sitting on the backs of her heels. "You understand that I *have* to punish you, don't you?" Burke began lowering the zipper to his trousers with his left hand while continuing to hold her hair with his right fist. When she didn't reply, he shook her head again, even more harshly than the first time. "Don't you?"

"Yes," Svetlana replied.

Burke had to struggle to pull his thoroughly aroused cock out through the fly of his trousers. When he was at last free, his erection throbbing with virility, he looked down at the stylishly dressed bound woman on her knees in front of him. For several seconds, he had to close his eyes to regain his composure. Svetlana's sensuality was as powerful as a narcotic and twice as dangerous.

He opened his eyes again and eased his hips forward. When the head of his cock touched her lightly painted lips, she squeezed them tightly together — in direct defiance of what she had to know was Burke's wishes.

"Open," Burke said, rubbing his cockhead back and forth over her lips, holding her hair with his right hand as he used his left to guide his erection. "Open." Finally, Svetlana did as he had commanded. "Wider." She opened her mouth a little more. "Wider!" To put emphasis to his demand, he gave her hair several harsh tugs.

Svetlana opened her mouth, and Burke thrust his cock between her lips and into the warm, wet confines of sexual paradise.

She's so beautiful. Burke was amazed at his astonishing good fortune. *On her knees with my cock in her mouth. Unbelievable. Simply unbelievable.*

After all these years, Burke can still fire up the heat. Svetlana sucked on the hard manly flesh that filled her mouth. *Only he can turn on the submissive in me.*

She leaned back slowly, dragging her lips over the cock's heavily-veined shaft, then over the plum-sized crown. Holding just the tip of his cock between her lips, she used her tongue against the slit. When she heard Burke groan, she had to suppress a smile. She knew he loved it when she pleasured him this way.

She resisted the urge to tilt her head back on her shoulders to look up into Burke's eyes. She wouldn't give in to that temptation just yet. It was always such an incredible turn-on for her to be tasting his cock, feeling it pulse and throb with lust between her lips and against her tongue, while she was looking up into his dark, fathomless eyes.

Burke groaned softly, the sound coming out from deep in his chest. It was a sound of pure pleasure, and Svetlana was overwhelmed with joy that when Burke was looking for pleasure, he was looking for her.

When she felt him release his hold on her hair, she experienced a momentary pang of regret. It aroused the submissive in her whenever he grabbed her by the hair and played the full-on hardcore Dominant to the max. A moment later, out of the corner of her eye, she watched as his hand-tailored suit coat fell to the floor. Burke was getting undressed — or at least as undressed as he ever allowed himself to be with her. He had lost his left foot just above the ankle and wore a prosthetic, and he was adamant that he would never allow Svetlana to see his injury. Though Svetlana wanted otherwise, she allowed Burke to keep his secrets . . . especially because she had no choice in the matter.

Seconds later, Burke's shirt with the button-down collar fell to the floor atop his jacket. Svetlana continued nodding slowly back and forth, sucking his cock with every ounce of fellatio skill that she possessed, but as she did, she allowed herself the satisfaction of tilting her head back on her shoulders. She looked up just in time to watch the fluid movement of muscles beneath a rather hairy chest as Burke pulled his T-shirt over his head.

My God, that's a beautiful body.

It wasn't the first time Svetlana had come to that conclusion. It wasn't the thirtieth or even the hundredth time. Still, whenever they were separated for days or even weeks because of a mission, it was the first thing that went through her mind when she looked at him. His body was *always* erotic to look at, but it was *especially* erotic to look at when her hands were tied behind her back, she was on her knees, and his beautiful cock was gliding slowly back and forth between her lips.

Burke began unbuckling his belt, and as he did so, he looked down into Svetlana's eyes. She trembled softly on her knees, looking at a man who could be merciful or merciless, depending upon the circumstance. Closing her eyes, Svetlana bobbed and weaved a bit faster, not certain what Burke wanted next from her. Even though they had something of a ritual whenever she returned from an assignment, Burke changed it up just enough so that she was never quite certain what was going to happen next.

Burke lowered his trousers to the middle of his thighs, then, struggling briefly, pulled back enough to release his erection from Svetlana's oral embrace to get his boxers down. Reaching down with his left hand, he grabbed a handful of Svetlana's hair as he took his cock in his right hand and raised it to his stomach, exposing the heavy, low-hanging egg-shaped testicles beneath.

"You know what to do," he said with quiet authority.

Shivering with desire, Svetlana angled her face somewhat sideways, then leaned forward and sucked one of his balls between her lips and into her mouth. Her eyes were closed, and she moaned softly. When Burke released the hold he had on his cock, the moist, pulsating shaft rested heavily on her cheek. As she sucked on Burke, she purred softly, like a hungry kitten drinking warm milk from a dish.

Releasing Burke, Svetlana licked her way slowly up to the crown, sucked on it for several seconds, then licked her way down the opposite side of the shaft. She took his other testicle into her mouth, basting it with her saliva as she felt her own juices flowing freely to the lips of her pussy.

"Enough," Burke said, and an instant later pulled hard on Svetlana's hair.

She gasped as she was catapulted to the side, her scalp tingling as several strands of hair were pulled out of it. She didn't stop moving until she was at the edge of the bed with her knees on the floor and her upper body on the mattress.

"Damn you, woman!" Burke said sharply. Svetlana felt her skirt being lifted to the small of her back and her panties get forcibly tugged down to the middle of her thighs. "Always needing punishing, always needing to be put in your place!"

An instant later she felt the crown of his cock touch the lips of her sex, then rub rather hurriedly up and down over her entrance. Once again, Burke filled a hand with her hair, but this time, as he pulled her head far back on her shoulders, he thrust his cock into her slick pussy.

"Awww!" Svetlana gasped. It was the only sound she could make with her neck stretched so tautly.

The next few minutes was a rollercoaster of emotions for Svetlana. Burke plundered her body, driving his cock between the lips of her pussy and deep into her body with furious energy, and as he did this, he put emphasis to each thrust by pulling on her hair. With his free hand he spanked Svetlana's ass cheeks.

Svetlana climaxed short moments later, her body rocking under the onslaught of Burke's hips striking the backs of her thighs and her buns, her cunt flexing around his plundering cock.

Oh, God, this time he's going to fuck me to death. She came down from the heights of that first wrenching orgasm, then realized that she was already escalating to another orgasm that showed promise of being even more powerful than the first.

She could hear Burke huffing like a steam engine behind her as he labored at his task of fucking her. She felt his pelvis pounding into her, knocking her against the side of the bed. But most of all she felt his cock — that great, big, beautiful giver of satisfaction — driving deep into her, filling her channel completely, forcing her body to accommodate both his length and girth.

Svetlana's second climax was, in fact, exactly as she had suspected it would be. It was as though a stick of dynamite had been detonated inside her body, and though her eyes were squeezed tightly shut, brilliant lights of red, blue, green, and white erupted like Fourth of July fireworks inside her skull.

And still he thrust into her. Relentless, forceful, driving full length, then withdrawing almost completely before plunging forward yet again.

This time he really is going to kill me. Svetlana felt a third orgasm beginning to form in the pit of her stomach. *I can't come again. I really can't. A woman can take only so much.*

She heard Burke's growl of ecstasy as he drove full-length into her cunt one more time, then stop, fully buried inside her hungry, receptive body. Svetlana knew that he was releasing his passion, and she was actually thankful that he had reached the zenith of pleasure when he had, because she wasn't at all certain that another climax wouldn't kill her.

With her cheek against the bedspread and her eyes closed, Svetlana whispered, "My God, Burke, how do you do it? Every time you fuck me, it's better than the last."

Two hours later, completely naked, unbound, and thoroughly

and gloriously sexually satisfied, Svetlana turned her face just enough to kiss Burke's naked chest. He still had his pants on, of course.

The Dominance and submission was always the first course when they got together after one of Svetlana's assignments. It involved game-playing and bondage and whatever Burke's incredibly erotic imagination could come up with. Then after that, there was the gentle, caring, slow lovemaking that sometimes took hours to complete.

Svetlana was perspiring, her body moist with a combination of her sweat and Burke's. Making sweet love with him was just as satisfying as being tied up and ravished, and in this encounter, she had received bountiful measures of both.

She licked the side of his chest and enjoyed the salty tang of his body, then asked, "So what's the mission?"

"There's a very dangerous, very nasty Ukrainian named Boris Antonich. Our government—Omega Force, that is—would like you to make him a very ugly, very dead corpse we no longer have to worry about."

CHAPTER TWO

Moscow, Russia

Major Dmitri Kuzetsov looked around at Moscow — *his* Moscow, he always privately thought, as though he ruled over it like a czar — and decided that it was the most beautiful city in the world. At least it was the city in which he most felt at home, and there weren't many major cities in the world where he hadn't already spent considerable time, even though he was just in his early thirties.

Ahead of him, still a good fifteen minutes away even walking at a brisk pace, was his destination. It was the headquarters of the Main Directorate of the General Staff of the Armed Forces of the Russian Federation. That cumbersome title was generally reduced to the GRU. The GRU was the great-grandchild of the infamous KGB of the former USSR days. The GRU was the largest of the intelligence forces of the Russian military command, and Dmitri was under the service of one of its most secret services, the Red Star Unit.

It was a glorious morning, with the rising sun shining ever-brightening rays as people hurried off to work, most of them taking the mass transit system, which in Moscow and St. Petersburg was one of the few governmental entities that worked with clockwork precision. Many, many other aspects of Moscow weren't nearly so efficient, mostly due to corruption within the political and business upper-class elites. When the USSR fragmented, many things that once had worked soon no longer did. Dmitri tried to not think too much about this. His reasoning, perhaps self-serving, was that there wasn't anything he could do about it, and if there wasn't, then why should he waste his time and energy dwelling on things he had no influence over?

As he walked nearer to the headquarters, his place of employment on Khoroshovskoye Shosse, he marveled at the beauty of the building. It had cost nearly nine and a half billion rubles to build, which was a fortune by any measure in any government on earth, but within its seventy-thousand square meters worked countless men and women in various branches of the GRU who toiled day and night for their country. Dmitri believed that the service they performed for Mother Russia was worth any price. That building was the equivalent of the Pentagon in the United States, and the things that went on there and the decisions that were made were just as important to Russia as those made in the Pentagon were for the United States.

Dmitri stopped his brisk stride as he was about to cross the street, because a transit bus came barreling past. The bus drivers in Moscow were notorious for their fast driving and their cavalier attitude toward the pedestrians they struck with their mammoth machines. Dmitri knew that this was because those drivers caught holy hell from their managers if they were so much as a minute late on their appointed rounds. The schedules, made by managers who had never spent a minute behind the steering wheel of a bus, were calculated for absolutely perfect driving conditions. Since perfection in Moscow for driving was never perfect, the drivers lived in a state of constant paranoia. They had the accelerator to the floorboard more often than not.

Also, by Russian standards, the drivers got paid rather handsomely. Many jobs were much more laborious and paid significantly less. It was incentive to stay on schedule.

Dmitri checked traffic both ways before he crossed the

street. Safe now on the other side, he looked up once again at GRU Headquarters. It never failed to please him to look upon that mammoth wonder of Russian architecture from a distance.

He wondered what the day would have for him. On most days, as he sat in his office at his desk in full uniform, he tapped away at his computer, searching for possible foreign enemies of Russia. He was always rather bored on those day. On other days, he was given an assignment to kill the enemies of Mother Russia. Those days never bored him.

General Igor Lebedev leaned back in his chair, took a sip of his coffee, then a second and third sip. He had to make room in the white ceramic cup that had been stained from years of use for the vodka. From the lower righthand desk drawer, the general pulled out a bottle of serviceable, locally-distilled vodka. It wasn't the finest vodka produced by Russia — the general was on a fixed military income, after all — but it wasn't bad, and that was good enough for him. He had reached the rank of general, but he was still a comrade in his soul. He unscrewed the cap, topped off his coffee cup, stirred the heated mixture with his forefinger, wiped his wet finger on the leg of his uniform, then returned the bottle to his desk drawer.

On mornings like this one, his psyche needed a little fortifying with Russia's most celebrated libation. He lit his twelfth cigarette of the morning — an American-made one using a blend of Turkish and Virginia tobacco. The cigarettes were without a filter. He didn't want anything to dilute his tobacco pleasure.

He was about to see his best field operative, Dmitri Kuzetsov. Not only was Dmitri the best at what he did — namely, killing people who were an imminent threat to Russia — he was the best at it *by far*. But he was also

16

temperamental in certain ways, and decidedly picky about the assignments he accepted. Very early in his career he had been assigned the task of killing a political rival of a popular politician in power who had been elected on a platform of law and order. The original order had been given, unironically, by a man being bribed by several other countries of the former USSR to look the other way when military arms and ammunition *went missing.*

Dmitri had refused the assignment. He stated he wouldn't kill a Russian for those reasons. He said that the GRU had enough assassins who didn't care who they killed or what the motive for their assassination was. Dmitri declared that he himself wasn't going to be an assassin without a worthy, patriotic motive. Then he marched out of General Lebedev's office, slamming the door behind himself.

But the next assignment he was offered — and he was now *offered* assignments, not given *orders* to do the assignment — was to hunt down and kill the terrorists in Chechnya that had resulted in the murder of dozens of innocent Russian children. Dmitri had accepted the mission, and for months afterward, the names of the terrorists responsible for the unspeakable atrocity would come up on General Lebedev's computer. Sometimes it was just one name a month, but at other times it would be one a week. On one particularly productive, vengeful, bloody day, six names of known terrorists came across the general's computer monitor. Dmitri had hit his stride, and the terrorists were falling by the score.

The general learned to never question Dmitri's methods. It didn't matter to the general how Dmitri accomplished his assignments, only that he carried them through to a successful conclusion. Every man that had been put on the hit list had been crossed off it, and no names *not* on the list had been hurt. That was all that really mattered, the general reasoned. As a military officer, he had always prided himself on being practical.

When Dmitri was on assignment, there was never the euphemistically titled collateral damage.

Still, it was sometimes quite difficult to be the commanding officer of a killer with a conscience and an unbending code of honor that he had written for himself and simply wouldn't violate under any circumstance. None of his other field agents had those parameters on their behavior.

So if the general had a particularly patriotic agent who refused to kill on the basis of politics, but had no qualms about unleashing his spectacularly lethal skills on terrorists and drug dealers plying their trade to the detriment of Russia, he simply had to learn to give commands within the framework of boundaries that Dmitri had set for himself.

The general was hoping like hell that Dmitri would accept the next assignment he was offered. The general had someone who Russia desperately needed to be stopped, and there was no one else in the world he could think of who was more capable of handling that task than Major Dmitri Kuzetsov.

How many people work here? Dmitri watched countless people—most in uniform, but many in civilian clothing, even though all of them were part of the Russian military—all hurrying to their offices. Some were number-crunching accountants the military brass always feared because they were afraid their budgets would be cut if the figures weren't favorable or the economy wasn't cooperating. Some were radio technicians who intercepted phone calls, mostly of Russian citizens but also of foreigners, particularly anyone working for a foreign government. Others were military analysts of one nature or another. But some of them were men like Dmitri. They were men who were trained to perfection to do one simple thing: kill a specific enemy as decided by the highest ranks of the Russian intelligence agency, the GRU.

For the official record, Dmitri's military specialty was to try to figure out what other countries were doing when they moved their troops around Europe. Specifically, his title was Satellite Photo Reconnaissance Analyst. For operatives of the Red Star Unit, though, the only real job was to neutralize enemies of the Russian Federation.

He saw the door to General Lebedev's office at the end of the long hallway, on the fourth floor of the building, and his heart skipped a beat. Was he about to be given an assignment? It had been nearly two months since his last one, so now he was getting bored and restless, and those were two emotions he worked hard to avoid.

He looked up at the video camera above the door, then thumbed the small door button near the door's brass knob. Several seconds passed before he heard the electronic "click" of the lock being released. He took the doorknob in his hand, inhaled deeply and exhaled slowly to calm himself and to buck up his optimism, then turned the knob and opened the door that led to the general's outer office, and which housed possibly the most efficient secretary in the world, Sergeant First Class Yelena Oblonsky.

Sixty seconds earlier, standing in the outer office of General Lebedev, was his secretary, Sergeant First Class Yelena Oblonsky. Standing in front of her was Private Kira Yahontov. She was nineteen, and had been in the military just over a year. She appeared to be a little nervous, and Yelena understood why.

"Continue," Yelena said, her tone quiet and yet still quite official, even authoritarian. She could feel her heart start beating just a little faster.

She watched, unblinking, as Kira hooked her thumbs into

her bikini panties, then eased them over the gentle curve of her hips. Bending at the waist, she brought the panties down to her ankles, then stepped out of them. Straightening, she handed them to Yelena, who slipped them onto the wooden hanger, which held the rest of Kira's military uniform, that of a private in the GRU's computer hacking program.

"Turn around," Yelena said quietly. "Turn around slowly."

Kira did as she had been ordered to. Her heart was pounding in her chest. She hadn't expected to be called to this office. In the past, several of her friends had been summoned here, but she never thought she'd get her turn. It was an honor, she knew, but still . . .

"Don't be frightened. He's masterful," the secretary said.

"I . . . I'm not really frightened. Just . . . I don't know what." She tried to moisten her lips with the tip of her tongue, but found that her mouth was so dry there wasn't enough saliva to accomplish the task. "Do you think he'll like me?"

With a cold rationality, she knew her physical positives and negatives—at least she thought she did. She was quite short, though, just barely over five feet tall, and she tried to think of her breasts as being pert, but an objective person would say they were really quite small. Since she didn't have a lot of curve to her hips, in her less-confident days she saw herself as being unattractively boyish. She'd always wanted to be voluptuously, extravagantly feminine, but that was not her fate.

One of the things she liked about being in the military was that the uniform she wore gave her body a bit more shape than normal civilian clothes, and she saw herself as being more mature while wearing it.

She wished now that she was still wearing her uniform instead of standing completely naked in General Lebedev's outer office, with his stern secretary looking at her with eyes that gleamed and an expression on her face that was completely unreadable.

A bell chimed softly, and Yelena touched a button on her desk. Kira heard the electronic lock on the door come unlatched. The door opened, and Kira's heart seemed to stop for a moment. She was standing toward the right side of the room, near the coat rack in the corner, so whoever had opened the door couldn't see her.

The secretary gave her a quick, amused smile, then hurried to the front of her desk, which faced the open door directly.

"Come in, Major Kuzetsov. The general's been anticipating your arrival, but he thought you might like to meet someone else first."

The man was Major Dmitri Kuzetsov. He stepped into the room and closed the door. He was every bit as handsome as Kira had been told that he was. Standing four inches over six feet, he had broad shoulders and a distinctly narrow waist. To look at his face, with its ice blue eyes, prominent nose, rather gaunt cheeks, and sensual mouth, she could tell that he didn't have an ounce of flab on his entire body. He did, however, have a lot of muscle.

When he looked at Kira, his gaze went slowly up and down in an assessing manner over her naked body. Then he looked at Yelena, and said, "It would seem I'm about to be sent on an assignment."

"Yes. The general, of course, didn't confide the details to me. He never does. But he did say that this could be a dicey one for you." Her eyebrows lifted for a moment. "Still, there are certain ancillary pleasures to be found in being given an assignment."

"Yes," Dmitri said. "Indeed."

Kira had little understanding of the subtext of what they were talking about, and she didn't know at all what she should do next or what was expected of her. She didn't know where to put her hands. Should she cover her sex in some semblance of modesty? What would the handsome officer who had walked into the outer office want her to do? What kind of demeanor did he like in a woman? Was she even womanly enough for his tastes? Kira wondered now whether she was fortunate or damned that she had won the lottery.

"How much time do I have?" the man Kira had been told was a force in the GRU asked the secretary. She wasn't at all certain what that meant.

"Not much, I'm afraid. This can't be your usual marathon." Once again, the secretary's eyebrows lifted briefly, then dropped with amusement. "Don't worry. I'll take over when you're finished."

Kira had no idea what that cryptic comment meant, but she suspected she would soon find out. She had the feeling that she was swimming in water *way* over her head.

When the gorgeous man turned toward her, a half-smile on his lips and mischief in his blue eyes, Kira, despite being completely naked, straightened to attention and snapped a smart salute to a superior office.

"Private Kira Yahontov awaiting your command, sir!"

My God, she looks young.

Dmitri let his eyes drink in the beautiful soldier's naked splendor.

"You don't need to salute," he said, the right side of his mouth pulling upward slightly in a hint of a smile. "Under the circumstances, it seems to me that we don't have to be quite so formal." The girl put her hand down at her side. Dmitri stepped closer. "You're sure you want to be here?" Dmitri always had to ask before things progressed very far. He'd never forced himself on anyone, and he sure as hell wasn't going to start now.

The girl nodded. Her eyes seemed very large and round to Dmitri. She cleared her throat softly, then said, "I put my name on a slip of paper, and then it was put into a hat with the names of the other girls. My name got picked." She smiled a bit demurely, then turned her gaze down, the faintest hint of a smile on her distinctly kissable lips. "I won the lottery."

"Well, as long as we're clear on that . . ."

He began to take off his uniform jacket, and Yelena extended a hand and took it from him. Then he started to toe off his black shoes, but the general's secretary said, "Sorry, Dmitri, you don't have time for all the niceties."

Dmitri made a face. He looked at the girl and said, "I'm sorry. I hope you won't be too disappointed."

He started to unbuckle his belt as Yelena placed his coat carefully on her desk, but the girl said swiftly, "No, don't do that." She sank fluidly to her knees, and with slender hands that trembled slightly, reached for his belt buckle. "Let me do it. I'm here to do whatever you want me to do."

She fumbled a little unfastening his belt. When she accomplished the task, she opened it, as well as the slacks of his uniform. Lastly, she pulled down his zipper very slowly.

Dmitri could tell she didn't have a lot of history in doing such things, and he made a mental promise to make this as pleasurable an experience as possible under the less-than-ideal time restriction.

Yelena walked around her desk and sat in the chair. As his trousers were lowered to mid-thigh, his white cotton briefs bulged. The secretary's gaze, Dmitri noted, was fixed on the completely naked young girl kneeling at his feet.

"Oh," the girl said quietly. "Oh, that's . . ." Her words died away.

The general's secretary said softly, ambiguously, "Beautiful."

Dmitri noticed that the secretary never once looked at him.

He wasn't in the least bit offended. He had more women than he could count coveting him, so he didn't feel a deficit because the general's oh-so-trusted secretary wasn't one of them.

Kira curled her fingers into the waistband of Dmitri's briefs, and he could tell she was summoning up courage to take the next step forward in this encounter. Part of him wanted to tell her that she could leave right now, if that was what she really wanted. He had never been a man to foist himself upon a woman. But another part of him — that virile, lustful part of him that was forever searching for a new sexual conquest — willed Kira to take the next bold step by freeing his cock, which by this time was nearly fully erect.

Like a person easing her way into very warm bath water that might scald her if she advanced too quickly, Kira pulled on the elasticized waistband of Dmitri's underwear. She exposed him slowly, her mouth opening slightly as an erection of significant dimensions was at last revealed to her.

"I thought the other girls were exaggerating," Kira said as she curled her slender fingers around the base of Dmitri's shaft. "But they weren't just making up stories. You really *are* this big."

From behind her desk, and in a tone of voice that held a slight undercurrent of pique in it, Yelena said, "The clock is ticking."

Dmitri watched as the girl brought her moist lips to the pulsing crown of his cock and planted several light kisses on it, then used the tip of her tongue against the sensitive underside of the crown. His cock instantly reached full stature. Reaching down, he cupped the back of her head in the palm of his left hand to hold her steady, then pushed his hips at her, slowly but with muscular determination. Her jaws opened, and her lips moistly caressed the head of his cock as it pushed deeper into her mouth. When she held the crown of his arousal in her mouth, Dmitri felt her begin to swirl her tongue against the underside, and he could tell that though she didn't have a lot of experience in being on her knees in front of a man, she certainly was no virgin. He was determined to be a significant person in the sharply upward pointing learning-curve of her sensual life.

"Yes, that's good," he whispered. *Life is good,* he thought as the girl on her knees he'd only met moments earlier began swanning her head and shoulders as she performed a slow blow job that Dmitri could savor like a libertine.

Kira closed her eyes, and a shiver went through her. She had never sexually done anything like this. Not even close to anything like this. She had stripped off her clothes and then waited — naked — for him to arrive. She was giving herself sexually to a man she did not know and had not even met until a few seconds earlier. She was performing a very lewd sex act upon the aforementioned man while a woman watched her.

My God, this is exciting.

She drew a slightly more powerful vacuum on the manly flesh that filled her mouth. She leaned toward Dmitri until she had the crown of his cock wedged against the opening of her throat, then she rotated her face around the bounty that was hers to enjoy herself with. She could hold barely a fourth of Dmitri's length in her mouth. A shiver of fear went through her. He was *big.*

"Ohhh. Oh, yesss."

Dmitri's softly spoken compliment delighted Kira, and made her want to pleasure him all the more.

"Remember, Dmitri, you don't have a lot of time," Yelena said with equal measures of warning and authority.

"I guess you'll just have to sit in the chair," Dmitri said, indicating the single, straight-backed wooden chair that faced the secretary's desk.

Kira leaned away from him, releasing him from her oral

embrace. She sat on the backs of her heels. She stroked his now saliva-moistened cock from the root to the head and back again. She looked up into his eyes, absolutely loved the passion she saw twinkling in the bottomless blue depths, then gave her head a little shake, sending her hair swirling over her shoulders.

"Not in the chair." She wasn't at all sure how much authority she had to make requests, but she was determined to at least make her wishes known. "Do it do me the way you did it to Anya." She saw Dmitri's eyebrows push together in confusion. Then she understood that he simply didn't remember Anya's name. Kira wondered just exactly how many lovers had tiptoed in and out of this handsome soldier's life. "You did it to her standing up against the door. She had bruises on her hips." She saw the sudden look of alarm register in Dmitri's eyes. He relaxed when she added, "She bragged about them for a month, but the bruises only lasted a week."

"If that's what you want, my darling girl," Dmitri said, reaching a hand down to Kira. "Then that's what I will give you."

She wanted to be the one whose name he remembered fondly, the one he thought of when his mind wandered and libidinous thoughts slithered sensually through his consciousness. She wanted her name to taste sweet on his lips long after this tryst was over.

She took his hand and allowed him to pull her to her feet. Barefoot and completely naked in front of Dmitri, she felt very small, very vulnerable — and oddly, for the first time ever, this made her feel very, very sexual. Dmitri was over a foot taller than she, and he surely weighed well over a hundred pounds more than she. Strength and power seemed to emanate from every pore in his body.

Dmitri bent at the waist, and Kira snaked her arms around his neck. She angled her head to the side, and almost immediately Dmitri's mouth, firm and commanding, sealed over hers. At the same time his broad-palmed hands slid down from her shoulder blades to cup the cheeks of her ass. His caress was both deft and muscular.

Kira opened her mouth invitingly, and immediately she received her reward as Dmitri's tongue slipped between her lips. Even from the very first instant, their tongues danced as though their movements had been choreographed, as though they had been kissing each other for years, instead of this being the first time in each other's arms. She felt his fingers, long and strong, squeezing her ass cheeks firmly for several seconds, then relax as his palms moved softly, caressingly over her flesh.

Kira moaned, but the sound of her passion was swallowed up with Dmitri's lusty kiss. All fear and uncertainty about what she was doing vanished as she savored that first long, deep, wanton kiss with Dmitri. When Kira suddenly felt cold hard wood against her heated naked back, she realized that Dmitri had been guiding her backward, though she hadn't even been aware of it at the time. She was now trapped between the door and Dmitri, and she felt both vulnerable and wickedly wanted.

He released his claim on her mouth, and by the time he did, Kira was panting with escalating desires that had hit her so quickly she was completely unprepared for them. He kissed her cheek next, then bent his knees so that he could use his lips on her throat.

"God," Kira gasped when she felt his lips and tongue caress the extremely tender and responsive skin of her neck. When he used his teeth to lightly nip at her throat, Kira let out a yip of surprise and approval. She loved the way Dmitri used his lips, tongue, and teeth on her throat while his hands explored the contours of her bottom. There wasn't any part of her body that wasn't aroused.

Dmitri kissed lower, moving his way to follow her collar-bone from right to left, using his lips and tongue on skin that Kira wasn't certain wouldn't simply burst into flame at any moment. Dmitri bent his knees even more, turning his attention lower on Kira's body.

He's going to kiss my breasts. Oh, please, please, please suck on my nipples, my darling barbarian.

Kira brought her hands from the back of Dmitri's neck to slide her palms over the top of his head, caressing his silky very short blond hair. She surprised herself when she tightened the hold she had on him, and rather forcefully — or was it more accurately *selfishly* — guided his mouth to her right nipple, which was tight and distended with passion.

Dmitri turned his head at an angle. She now watched him, in perfect profile, as he opened his mouth wide, then sucked all of her nipple and areola between his lips. Kira cried out in passion and tossed her head back on her shoulders, forgetting that she was against the door. Her head banged loudly against the solid wood, and for several seconds she had colored lights of red and green flashing and blinking in the backs of her eyes.

She didn't care if she ended up with a bump on the back of her head the size of a goose egg. All that mattered was that a supremely handsome well-endowed, virile man was sucking on her nipple — and that every sensually responsive nerve in her body was vibrantly, intensely alive.

The secretary said, "Dmitri, you mustn't forget about the time." Kira could hear concern in her voice, and something else, though she couldn't say what it was.

Shut up, damn you. You're just an old hag.

Kira was angry, but immediately felt guilty for her uncharacteristic and uncharitable thoughts. The secretary was perhaps twenty years older than Kira, but still was by no means a "hag." But the last thing in the world that Kira wanted was for this encounter to end. Not in ten minutes. Not in ten hours.

Not in ten days.

Dmitri released her nipple from between his lips, then got down on one knee in front of Kira. He looked up to her face, and the glittering quality in his icy eyes let her know his lust was galloping in thoroughbred strides with nostrils flared and long legs eating up the distance to the finishing line.

His hands moved, surprising Kira as they went from the globes of her bottom, around to the insides of her thighs, then moved between her legs, his elbows parting her thighs as his hands once again cupped her ass.

"What—" Kira gasped, but could manage no more of a question than that.

An instant later, Dmitri got both feet beneath him, then stood to his full height of six-foot-four inches—and he took Kira with him. He shifted her so that the backs of her thighs were first on his forearms, and then on his biceps, with his arms straight out in front of him and his palms pressed flat against the door.

Kira was sitting on his arms with her legs spread wide, the top of her head very nearly touching the office ceiling. Her most intimate place was very near his mouth. She knew this wasn't an accident or mere spectacular serendipity. He had planned this, she could tell. *Anything you want of me is yours to take.*

She looked down into Dmitri's eyes, and he said, "Give it to me. Give me your pussy."

It was a command that Kira didn't have to be given twice. She wiggled a bit on his biceps, and a moment later her seething pussy was pressed against Dmitri's mouth.

The first thing she felt was his tongue getting thrust between the sex lips. She forced herself to keep her eyes open, because she didn't want to miss anything—not one single sensory thing—that Dmitri was doing to her. She could *feel* him, but she wanted to *see* him as well. Her sensory delight was both visual and tactile.

Under any circumstances, Dmitri was a handsome man. As a woman, Kira had understood this from the very beginning. But *never* had she imagined that he could look so handsome . . . with his head between her thighs and his mouth pressed tightly against her cunt. His nose was buried in the sparse, soft, curly hair of her pubis. She couldn't see anything of him from his nose downward, but that was okay with her, since that which she couldn't see was busy giving her the most electrifying pleasure that she had ever known.

She looked around the room, her mind in a whirl, coherent thoughts almost impossible to grasp. It took a while for her to fully comprehend that she was sitting on Dmitri's arms, that she was many feet above the floor . . . and that an orgasm was approaching that would wash over her like a tsunami.

She looked down once again at the incredibly sexually talented and decadent man who was currently delivering the kind of tongue lashing that every woman craved but few actually had the courage to demand. And even when they did, they were more often than not disappointed in what they received.

Oh, yes . . . he's that good. He's as good as all the girls say he is.

Suddenly, rather than licking her, Dmitri captured her erect clit between his lips, and he began sucking on it lightly as he used his tongue on it. The sensations this action created within Kira's sex and throughout her entire body were electrifying.

"Oh, God," she whispered, then put a fist to her mouth to silence any further comments.

A moment later she felt her insides all contract. Her legs straightened out at the knee, and her hands flew to Dmitri's head to hold him demandingly, forcing him to press his mouth even more tightly to her erupting cunt.

She seemed to teeter on the brink of a climax for hours, but her logical mind told her that it was really only a couple seconds. And then—for just the last couple seconds—what was supreme pleasure became something very akin to pain.

But then she started to come. She came harder and more forcefully than ever before in her life. The first contraction hit her like a fist in the lower stomach, and she bent forward, clutching even more desperately onto Dmitri's head. The second and third spasms immediately followed the first, though they were not quite as powerful. The fourth spasm was delayed for several more seconds than the others, but when it shuddered through her overheated body and senses, the pleasure it brought was nothing less than sublime.

"No," Kira said, almost sobbing, as she pushed against Dmitri's forehead to get his mouth away from her satiated and way-too-sensitive pussy. "No . . . more." She straightened, then leaned back against the wall, still sitting on Dmitri's powerful arms. "Fuck," she said, though she seldom used that word. "I thought I was going to turn inside out. I thought I was going to die."

With her head against the wall and her face tilted slightly upward, she closed her eyes and for several seconds simply breathed in and out deeply. She felt as though she desperately had to compose her senses and regain some semblance of control over her own life, her own world.

It was Yelena's voice, once again, that tore through her consciousness like a serrated knife wielded by a sadistic madwoman.

"The general's going to be furious with you if you don't get into his office right away," she said. "Dmitri, this is important. I told you that you didn't have much time. I said that before you even got started."

"Yes, yes, I know," Dmitri answered. He tilted his head up, looking into Kira's eyes, and she saw that his lips, cheeks, and chin were all slick and shining with the juices of her unbridled passion. "I've got to go." He closed his eyes, and seemed to shake his head at the injustice of the moment. "I'm sorry . . .

but I've got to go."

"But you promised me bruises," Kira said, her tone nothing more than a plaintive whisper. She knew she sounded very much like a little girl who was being denied a promised, savory chocolate. She was willing to beg to get what she needed. "The girls won't believe me if I don't have bruises." A sob caught in her throat. "They'll think you didn't want me and that I just made everything up." She reached down, and with the fingertips of both hands, touched Dmitri's face lightly. "Just a few bruises . . . and then I promise I'll never ask for anything more."

Dmitri began to lower Kira, easing his arms out from beneath her legs, one at a time, so that she could wrap her legs around his midsection while he supported her weight by putting his hands under her bottom. She put her arms once again around his neck. She found his immense strength exhilarating. He could manipulate her body as though she weighed nothing at all.

He lowered her body another couple inches, and then she felt the warm, hard shaft of his cock touching her. Several quiet, uncomfortable seconds passed. She didn't know what to say or do.

"Kira, you've going to have to help me," Dmitri explained. "I need both hands to hold on to you."

"I'm such a fool," Kira said as she unlaced her fingers from the back of Dmitri's neck, then reached down, wedging her right hand between their bodies.

"A beautiful, erotic, sexy, lovely fool," Dmitri amended.

She wrapped her fingers around the shaft of his cock, then angled it so that the throbbing crown was pressed against the lips of her entrance.

My God, he feels big. Almost immediately she felt Dmitri begin to push his hips forward.

For several seconds she wasn't certain her body would

open to accept Dmitri—she'd never before had sex with a man as endowed as he—but then her body permitted the invasion, and though she felt an initial slight twinge of discomfort, that sensation lasted only a couple seconds.

She cleared her throat and looked into Dmitri's eyes as he lowered her left leg so that she had one foot on the floor and one knee up in the crook of his elbow, and said with more sincerity in her tone of voice than she'd ever before had, "Remember, I said bruises, and they've got to last at least a week." She kissed Dmitri on the tip of his chin. Standing on one foot, she couldn't reach his lips. "Fuck me hard. I want bragging rights."

What happened next shocked Kira, because nothing in her life had ever given her any forewarning of just what it would be like.

Dmitri unleashed the full extent of his lustful passion on Kira, and in doing so, he gave her the bruises that she had quietly and a bit embarrassingly asked for. He straightened his legs, thrusting forward and upward simultaneously, and in doing so, drove the full length of his mighty cock into Kira's entrance.

"Oh, God!" she gasped as she was slammed backward against the door, lifted onto the tiptoes of the one foot that remained on the floor. The breath was forced from her lungs.

Dmitri retreated until just the tip of his cockhead was still separating the lips of her pussy, then he charged forward again, even more forcefully on this his second full-length plunge. His cock drove into Kira's tender body, but then it continued, and when his pelvis slammed against her and moved forward and upward, she was driven higher, and the one foot she had on the floor now dangled several inches above the carpeting.

Dmitri growled, the sound coming from deep within his broad chest. His powerful body pinned Kira against the door, his cock filling her completely before his hurried retreat. She held onto him tightly, her arms around his neck, one leg around his body, his arm beneath her knee, the breath rushing from her lungs when she was driven backward against the door.

Again and again Dmitri thrust into Kira, and with each full-length immersion into her body, she was lifted so that the one foot she had *wasn't* on the floor.

Kira started screaming when the next orgasm gripped her soul. She screamed into Dmitri's ear as her body convulsed, her pussy flexing around the rock-solid cock that seesawed back and forth between the lips of her cunt. The contractions within her were more powerful than anything she had ever before experienced, infinitely more wrenching than the orgasmic spasms that she created with her own fingers or the small, battery-operated vibrator that she sometimes used to give herself some semblance of peace and sexual tranquility when she was alone and feeling achingly empty of sexual satisfaction.

She could feel his strength, his virility, each time his cock filled her, each time his chest crushed her breasts and tantalized her nipples, which were pebble-hard and more erect than they ever before had been.

She came a second time, with a mere five more strokes of Dmitri's cock into her passion-hungry cunt, and as she was climaxing, she heard Dmitri's leonine growl of ecstasy, and knew that he was releasing his passion deep inside her.

For several seconds after Dmitri had stopped his relentless thrusts, he held Kira pinned against the door, her naked toes twitching inches off the floor. She could feel every inch of his erection pulsing inside her, feel every ounce of his strength as he pressed her against the door. When he released the hold he had on her leg, then lowered her, she placed both of her bare feet on the utilitarian carpeting.

"God," she whispered. "I can't see them yet, but I'm sure I'll have bruises." She kissed Dmitri's chest through his shirt. "Now I can brag for weeks and weeks." She felt Dmitri's cock slip out from between the lips of her pussy, and she sighed unhappily. "The first thing I'm going to do is put my name on a slip of paper, and put it back into the hat. There's a lot of names in there, but maybe my name will get picked again." She tilted her head back on her shoulders and looked up into Dmitri's eyes. "You'll want me again, won't you?" She heard the hunger in her tone, the need, the want.

"Yes," Dmitri said.

Kira closed her eyes, and pressed her cheek against his shirtfront. "Thank God." She let her fingertips run over his hair, and along his ears and cheeks. "Anytime you want me you can have me. Anytime. Any way you want me, I'm yours for the taking. You don't have to wait for the lottery."

CHAPTER THREE

"His name is Boris Antonich, and he's bad," General Lebedev said, lighting yet another cigarette with a wooden sulfur match as he looked at Dmitri through a cloud of smoke. "Ukrainian. Made his first fortune when he was cozying up to the Venezuelan government there. He was a suck-up to a high-ranking minister in the energy sector, and the oil reserves there are enormous. He was bootlegging oil by the tanker to various countries on the U.S. blacklist. Computer records and paperwork in the country were so sloppy that the bastard made millions, and nobody in the government figured out there was a drop of oil unaccounted for. Then he made a connection in China, and that's where he got into the fentanyl business. China had the means of production, and he had the means of distribution in more countries than we know about. A marriage made in hell."

Dmitri shrugged his shoulders noncommittally. "That's China and Venezuela for you."

That wasn't the tone of voice the general had hoped for with his most effective assassin. "True. But he's an ambitious man . . . and he's started to make inroads into Mother Russia. He likes seaport cities. All those boats and tankers he's used over the years, I suppose." General Lebedev saw fresh, glittering interest come into Dmitri's icy eyes. *This* was the body language he had hoped to see. "We didn't know what he was up to until he'd already brought his third big shipment into St. Petersburg. By then, one hell of a lot of damage had already been done."

He stubbed out his cigarette in a clear glass ashtray the size of a dinner plate on his desk. "This one's got a personal edge to it, Major. Fentanyl has killed a lot of people, but in this case, it killed two in particular that have gotten our attention. General Vlad Haakov had twin sons attending the University of St. Petersburg. They went to a party and fentanyl was there. They both took some and both of them died. One died that night, and one the next morning."

With his fist to his mouth, General Lebedev cleared his throat. "I've known General Haakov for nearly forty years. Hell, we were just kids in military school together. The death of his sons has devastated both him and his wife." A muscle twitched in General Lebedev's cheek. "We've trailed that son of a bitch to the Ukraine. Kiev. He always keeps bodyguards around him, and being home in Ukraine, he's not going to be easy to get to."

"I'll get him," Dmitri said, rising to his feet. "I just need the specifics."

"We haven't any clout in the Ukraine. Not the way it's between lately between us and them, so watch yourself, Dmitri." The general was distinctly aware of the fact that he'd just used the young soldier's Christian name. He did that only on the rarest of occasions.

"Yes, sir."

Kiev, Ukraine

Boris Antonich leaned back in his office chair and sipped his whisky and soda, thinking that it had been a pretty good day. It had started with an exciting ménage a trois with his two young mistresses, and that always put a nice glow on the beginning of a morning. It was shortly after noon that he had completed negotiations with his Chinese supplier for a new shipment of fentanyl. This time he had ordered two million pills of the narcotic, doubling the order of his first shipment. He didn't quite get the volume price cut he had hoped for, but he was still quite pleased with both the quality and the price. When he sold the pills to the various dealers he worked with, he'd make a fortune—and this was just the beginning of his profits. When he started distributing through western Europe, and more in South America, Mexico, Canada, and most importantly, the United States, his fortune would dwarf the cocaine kingpins in Bolivia and Mexico.

If this shipment went well, on his next order he would quadruple the size of his order, but he'd add just a little rat poison to perhaps one in twenty pills. He liked the idea of poisoning Americans, but he also needed to have repeat customers, so he had to make most of the pills provide their intended high. Most of his consumers *would* get high, but some would get low—as in six feet under the ground. He liked the odds . . . and he liked the profit.

He swiveled his chair to look out the floor-to-ceiling windows that gave him such a beautiful view of the prosperous business district in Kiev. While other sections of the city were showing great signs of neglect and disrepair, the accelerating decline of which had started with the fall of the Soviet Union, this part of the city was thriving.

I love this city more than any in the world. I love this country more than any in the world. He then took another swallow of his cocktail. *This is the one country in all the world where everything—every man, woman, child, and institution—is for sale. The only language that everyone here understands is money, and God knows, I've got plenty of that, and soon, I'm going to have much, much more.*

There was a soft knock on his office door. Boris was inclined to tell whoever was there to go away—he was enjoying his quiet contemplation—but it could be something important. People in his world knew that he wasn't to be disturbed unless it was important.

"Come in," he called out, this time turning his chair so that he faced his desk and the door at the opposite end of the room.

Yulia and Roma stepped in, the first one of them blonde and petite, the other with hair as black as coal and voluptuous curves that had caught Boris's attention the first time he'd seen her and had kept his attention ever since. She had said she had gypsy blood flowing in her veins. That significantly heightened his interest in bedding her, though he wasn't certain why. He often didn't understand why he desperately needed to fuck a girl. He always did fuck them. He always made sure of that. He just sometimes didn't understand why fucking them was so necessary. Afterward, once he'd had his orgasm, he often found himself confused by his ardent licentious need, though this was something he never really thought about for more than just a minute or two.

"Hello, Boris," the curvaceous one said, "can we talk to you for a moment?"

"Of course, my sweet. After the way you treated me this morning, how can I possibly deny you any request?"

It was a bald-faced lie. The two women, both twenty, had sex with him whenever he wanted it, whether they were in the mood or not. Their mood was of no concern to him. Their satisfaction was of no concern, either. They were as replaceable to him as the gasoline in his limousine, a commodity that needed replenishing every so often, and was then never again thought of.

Roma and Yulia stepped deeper into the room. Boris could see that they were dressed to go out into the city. Whenever they did, it always cost him money.

"We'd like to go shopping, to get some new, pretty clothes to wear so that you can see us in them," Roma said. She raised her eyebrows briefly. "We thought you'd like to see us lounging around in pretty bras and panties, or sexy nighties."

Bullshit. Boris knew that whenever he gave them money,

they bankrolled at least half of it, but told him they'd spent all of it.

"So you need money," Boris replied, already reaching for the wallet in the inside breast pocket of his robin's egg blue silk suit coat. "How much this time?" Roma gave him a figure, and Boris was surprised—but not for long—at her greed. "They'd better be some sexy underwear for me to shell out that much."

"They will be," the young woman replied, stepping forward, already putting out a hand with the palm upward.

"But there's something I need the two of you to do for me before you go pampering yourselves." He extracted his long, leather wallet and began removing large denomination paper bills. When he looked up, he saw that Roma and Yulia were staring at the money in his hand. "I want you to do for my men what you did for me this morning."

"What?" Yulia exclaimed, her mouth staying open when she'd voiced the single word. "You're joking, right?"

Boris just looked her directly in the eyes. His face was void of expression.

A heavy silence filled the office.

The voluptuous Roma, always the more practical of the two, broke the quietude by saying, "If that's what you want, then of course, that's what we'll do." She turned to her colleague. "Won't we?"

Boris caught the undercurrent of threat in Roma's tone to Yulia and liked it. "I want the two of you to do them one at a time. Give them the works—everything you've got. I want them happy. You make them happy, and I make you happy." He held out the money, and Roma quickly took it. "Do that now. And send Arkady in. I need to speak with him. You two can start with Vasily. He's probably in the game room. He does love his video games, doesn't he? And there's a nice sofa in that room. That should be good enough for your purposes.

Go now."

The young women left Boris's office without a backward glance. They'd been with Boris a little over a month, which was quite a long time for women to be in Boris's immediate circle.

Arkady stepped into the office a short time later. He was not a particularly large man, standing several inches under six feet, and he wasn't very broad across the shoulders and chest. But what he lacked in size, he made up for with sheer savagery and unwavering loyalty. Those were traits that Boris greatly admired in a man. If Boris gave the order, Arkady would kill anyone at any time. If Boris wanted the killing to be slow and painful, or quick as lightning and without a warning, Arkady was willing to accommodate his master's wishes.

"Yes, sir?" Arkady stepped up to the desk and stopped. "You sent for me?"

"Roma and Yulia have begun to think beyond their station in life, and I find that disturbing and disappointing. They're going to satisfy you, Vasily, and Joseph, and then they'll want you to take them out shopping. I've given them a small fortune in cash." Boris looked directly into Arkady's brown, expressionless eyes. "Retrieve my money, then sell them to Makari Pallinov. He's always looking for fresh young talent to put on the open market."

"Yes, sir," Arkady replied, with no more emotion than if he'd just been given a grocery list of items that his employer needed picked up. He turned and headed for the door.

"Wait a second, Arkady," Boris said quickly. "I just had a thought." His top bodyguard turned toward him. Boris noticed that his suit coat was tailored so perfectly that there wasn't a sign of the big-bore pistol in the holster under his left arm. "Rather than selling them, why not give them as a peace offering to Makari? He and I have been growling at each other for a while now. What do you think? Tell him I want to thaw the ice that's formed between us, and that those two girls should provide some heat to do just that."

Boris surprised himself by asking Arkady's opinion. He generally never cared for anyone's opinion but his own.

After several seconds, the right side of Arkady's mouth curled upward slightly. "I think it's a brilliant move. Makari will take that as a show of respect." His eyes narrowed fractionally and became just a little brighter. "He'll be less inclined to see you as a rival, and maybe more as a business partner."

"Just what I want him to think. If he ever lets his guard down, I'll want you to kill him and his men for me."

"I assumed as much, sir."

"Get my money, then get rid of the girls immediately. Then we'll be going to the People's Hotel. I'm going to need new companionship." He smiled coldly. "And do with the girls whatever you want, but don't leave any marks. I'd don't want them bruised or cut. I don't want to give Makari damaged goods."

"Don't worry, sir. I'll do what I want to do, and I won't leave any marks."

"And regarding the families of the girls, I want you to tell them that they're all going to have a picnic on the yacht, and that they'll get to see their girls. The families have been well-paid every week since the girls have been here?"

"Yes, sir. Every Friday."

"Good. Then they'll suspect nothing when they get on the boat." He looked away for a moment, but only a moment. "When you're far enough out to sea, turn them into shark food. Weight the bodies. I don't want corpses washing ashore."

"I'll take care of it myself, sir."

Boris knew about Arkady's streak of sadism. It was one of

the traits that made him so valuable to Boris. He was loyal as a German shepherd, and he loved his work.

Kiev, Ukraine

Dmitri was at the People's Hotel, this time playing a hunch rather than tailing Boris all around Kiev. Boris and his men would stop at this hotel bar, or that high-end watering hole, but only stay for a single drink before moving on. Eventually, they always ended up at the nightclub in the People's Hotel, where he had more than a single cocktail and ordered a meal. For two nights in a row, Boris and his three bodyguards had spent at least two hours at the hotel's nightclub. It wasn't hard to tell that Boris was scoping out women, and since there were plenty of provocatively clad young women in attendance and middle-aged men in tailored suits, all present seemed to know what the unwritten rules of the game were.

The People's Hotel was very much upscale in a country that was very corrupt and anything but upscale. At least that was the way it was for everyone but the elites of society. This truly was a country where the one-percenters had ninety-nine percent of the wealth. And since Boris was one of the one-percenters, Dmitri figured that was just the way he liked it.

From across room, Dmitri watched as the doorman pulled the velvet rope aside to allow Boris and his men to enter. The doorman moved more quickly for Boris than he did for other guests of the exclusive nightclub. Dmitri was pleased that he'd taken the assignment. Boris seemed like a man who needed to be put in his place . . . and that place was in a coffin six feet under the ground.

The three men with Boris had that hard look of men who knew first-hand what violence was, and almost always, they were on the distributing end of the violence, not the receiving end. When they sat at the plush booth that had space enough for six, the three bodyguards sat on one bench, and Boris sat by himself on the opposite. There could be no confusion regarding who gave the orders and who took them without question or hesitation.

Dmitri saw that one of the bodyguards — the smallest of the three, but the one who looked around the most — looked directly at him. Dmitri looked down at the glass of whiskey and ice in his hand, swirled the contents around several times, then swallowed it in a single gulp. He set the glass down on the round table in front of him before rising from his chair, making it seem as though he was having difficulty getting his feet securely planted beneath him. He blinked his eyes several times, then rubbed them, and finally, to end the theatrics, he inhaled deeply several times before letting his breath out very slowly one final time.

Weaving just a little bit, pretending that he was in the twilight zone between being slightly intoxicated and being thoroughly drunk, he left the nightclub.

He had learned everything he needed to know. Tomorrow night, he'd get in his rental car and follow Boris wherever he and his men went. If they presented him with the opportunity to end the assignment somewhere else, he'd take it. If he had to end the assignment in a crowded nightclub, he'd take that chance, too. But either way, on the next day, the assignment would end . . . with Boris as dead as if he had never been borne.

Tomorrow, Dmitri would be well-dressed in a rather expensive suit with a nice necktie, just as he was tonight. Only tomorrow, beneath his immaculately-tailored suit coat, he'd be wearing a figure-eight clamshell holster, and beneath his left arm would be a Beretta 9 mm. fitted with a detachable silencer to the muzzle.

Tomorrow would be Boris's last day of life. He just didn't know it yet.

Boris had killed many Russians with the poison called fentanyl. His soul now had upon it a great burden, a heavy debt. And for Mother Russia, Dmitri was about to collect on that debt.

Igor Sikorsky Kiev International Airport – Kiev, Ukraine

When Svetlana stepped out of the jetway into the airport in Kiev, the first thing she saw was a liveried chauffeur holding up a sign in front of his chest that read, in both English and Russian, "Madam Simonov".

She walked up to the man and said in English, but with a significant Russian accent, "I am Svetlana Simonov."

"I am with the Hotel International. Please, let me escort you to the limousine. I have a man waiting to retrieve your luggage." He gave her a smile that was professional, but just a little too pre-planned to be natural. "There is food and libation waiting for you in the car. Sometimes the traffic causes delays, but I will get you to Hotel International as quickly as possible."

"You're a jewel, my darling," Svetlana said with a theatrical exhausted sigh. It had taken some years, but she now understood how the very wealthy liked to feel themselves victimized when they had to suffer the slightest inconvenience. "It feels like I've been on this plane or that one for the last two weeks, and I am so looking forward to being pampered by your hotel's staff."

As they headed toward the limousine, the driver said, "At the Hotel International, we pride ourselves in our ability to pamper our guests, madam."

"It's *miss*, not *madam*. I'm not married," Svetlana said with just the slightest hint of upper-class disapproval.

"My apologizes, miss. I meant no offense."

"And I took none." Svetlana sighed expressively once

again. "You're sure there's libations in the car?"

"A bottle of Dom Perignon of a rather favorable year is opened and on ice, miss," the chauffeur said. "There's also chilled strawberries and whipped cream waiting for you."

"I think I'm going to love this city," Svetlana said.

"I can't speak for the city, only for Hotel International," the driver replied quietly. "But we try very hard to not disappoint women of your . . . caliber."

Damn, he's good. Svetlana wondered just how much he was getting paid by the hotel to say things like that to women like her. She hoped it was a considerable sum. He seemed like a decent fellow, and in the last decade, Svetlana had met very few of those.

Boris inhaled deeply, sighed softly, then looked out at the twinkling lights of Kiev. He hadn't had sex since his morning romp several days ago with the last girls he had moved into his two-story luxury apartment. Now he could hardly remember their names. He was a man who liked to have sex once a day — and that was the rock-bottom limit. Twice a day was nice. And sometimes, particularly on a Saturday, he liked to have sex three times.

Lately, the women who had been at the haunts where he usually found his lovers/mistresses hadn't sparked his interest. Was he getting picky as he got older? Yes, he told himself, he was getting more particular about the women he wanted to spend more than just an hour or two with. But still, he found it just a little odd that he hadn't simply chosen one of the young girls at the bar for a one-night romp. Usually he was a man who understood the concept of *any port in a storm*.

Tomorrow, no matter what, I find someone and she comes back here. He closed his eyes, took a sip of his drink, and swirled the liquor around his mouth with his tongue, savoring the taste and taking great pleasure in it. *Tomorrow, I own the world . . . and everyone in it.*

CHAPTER FOUR

Svetlana had chosen her clothes carefully for this day. She selected an Italian fashion designer who was famous for the youth of his male lovers and the boldness of his latest styles for women. He was a man who set out in a direction, then watched as the rest of the pack followed his lead.

On this day she wore a black miniskirt of sheer silk. Since it was almost guaranteed that she'd flash someone at some time or other during the day, she wore black bikini panties. She did not wear a thong, because she found them uncomfortable, though she owned several pairs, just in case she had a mark who liked to see her in them. Beneath the miniskirt she had decided to go without her usual thigh-high silk stockings, because the skirt was too short. Below the miniskirt was a pair of red-soled shoes with five-inch stiletto heels. When she wore them, she stood an intimidating six-foot-two. They cost more than most Ukrainians made in six months. Above the miniskirt was a red silk blouse that was rather loose-fitting. Beneath that was a bra that matched her panties and was made to be functional and beautiful at the same time. The jacket matched her miniskirt, and the bottom hem of it lined up perfectly with the bottom hem of her miniskirt.

The jacket had been altered slightly from the famous designer's original creation. The insides of the front two pockets were lined with firm elk-skin leather. The leather had been sewn there so that whatever was inside the pocket would not leave a bulge in the silk that could be discerned. This was important, because inside the right pocket of her oh-so-chic

48

jacket was a palm-sized, intricately engraved, gold-plated Browning pistol, in .25 caliber. Inside the left pocket was her small wallet containing her international driver's license, a half dozen credit cards that were accepted worldwide and had no limits on them, and a small money clip that held dollars, pounds sterling, euros, and other currency. Svetlana never really knew just how much money she was carrying with her at any given time. There was also a gold-plated smart phone, as ornately engraved as the pistol, and her passport.

It was three blocks from the hotel where Svetlana was staying to the hotel she knew that Boris Antonich frequented. She wasn't expecting him for a while yet, but that didn't bother her. In her profession, sitting around doing virtually nothing was much more common than the pulse-pounding I-could-die-at-any-moment type of violence that filled movie theatres showing action films.

As she walked along the boulevard, she was aware of the looks she was receiving, both from men and women. When the men were with women, they tried to hide their interest in her. Sometimes the wives noticed, and they jabbed their elbows into the sides of their wealthy but middle-aged husbands. In one case, walking on the sidewalk toward her, there was a rather old but obviously well-to-do man with a woman perhaps thirty or thirty-five years his junior on his arm. She was elegantly tall, though not quite as tall as Svetlana, and she was wearing around her neck a chain of gold, with alternating diamonds and emeralds.

During the last decade — in other words, during her time as an Omega Force agent — Svetlana had seen extraordinary wealth. But nothing she had ever before seen could match the beauty — and the obvious value — of the necklace around the woman's neck, resting on the full, upper swells of her pale breasts.

When Svetlana made direct eye contact with the woman as

they walker closed to each other, the woman gave her a half-smile. Svetlana's first thought was the expression was somewhat condescending, the woman pleased that another woman was obviously shocked at the stunningly expensive jewelry her husband was willing give her. But then, after a second or two, Svetlana realized that the gleam in the woman's eyes was sexual in nature, not imperious.

Oh, my. A frisson of emotion shot up Svetlana's spine. *I wonder if her husband knows.*

They passed each other, and Svetlana felt her heart beat just a little bit faster for perhaps less than a minute. She could picture the situation with the couple, the man too old to satisfy his much younger wife sexually, though still unwilling to let some young stud take his place in the bedroom. But he might not have such a critical attitude if she found her sexual relief in the arms of another woman—especially not if he was allowed to watch.

Concentrate on the mission.

Svetlana criticized herself for letting her thoughts tarry into libidinous territory when there were so much more important things to concern herself with.

She glanced at her wristwatch and saw that it was just now five o'clock. She wasn't expecting Boris and his men until at least seven o'clock.

Boris looked at the entrance to the hotel and wondered if he should just lower his standards a little, and pick up whatever pretty girl happened to be at the bar. Any way he looked at it, someone was better than no one. On very few occasions in the past two dozen years or so of his life had he found himself without a woman at his ready beck and call.

It was an awareness he did not like at all.

To the left of the five steps that led up to the entrance lobby to the hotel, at ground level with the street, was a small outdoor café with a dozen small, round tables, each with white table cloths and four chairs. Three of the tables were occupied, and the two waitresses serving the patrons were sitting on stools near the cash register. They had bored expressions on their faces. Obviously, neither was all that interested in having a conversation with the other.

"Arkady, let's drink and dine outside tonight," Boris said. "The weather is beautiful, and maybe my luck will be better with the fresh air."

Arkady nodded almost imperceptibly, but said nothing. He walked in front of Boris, with Vasily and Joseph walking behind their employer. Arkady opened the waist-high iron gate that surrounded the café and separated it from the foot traffic on the sidewalk that passed along the busy street.

Boris waited until Arkady pulled out a chair before he sat at a table. One waitress—in her middle-twenties, with fiery red hair, very pale skin, and a blizzard of freckles across the bridge of her nose—got up off the stool she was sitting on near the cash machine, and started forward. When Boris looked at her, he saw that she had sized up his expensive tailored silk suit and figured he had money, and the faint curl of her lipstick-brightened mouth let him know that she wanted a share of that fortune and was willing to do whatever was necessary to get it.

But even though Boris had gone several days without a woman, he wasn't interested in the waitress, no matter how eager she might be. He'd never really liked redheads, and he certainly didn't like them with freckles.

"Can I help you gentlemen?" she asked. Though she spoke to all four men, she looked only at Boris.

"What is your best whiskey?" Boris asked, his gaze going leisurely up and down over the young woman's figure. He made no effort at all to hide either the direction of his gaze or his disinterest.

51

She gave him the names of several American and Canadian whiskies, and from them Boris chose a Canadian. He always avoided anything American, except their currency. He ordered a double, with ice. Arkady ordered a tonic with a wedge of lime. Once he had made his decision, Vasily and Joseph ordered the same. None of Boris's bodyguards ever drank alcohol when they were on duty, unless they were given specific permission to do so.

When the waitress returned with the drinks, movement out of the corner of his eye caught Boris's attention. Was it movement, he asked himself a moment later, or had it been masculine instinct that caused him to turn toward the glass door that led from the hotel to the outdoor bar? Boris suspected the latter. At least he hoped it was.

She was very tall, he noted immediately, and her legs seemed to go on somewhere beyond forever. She had blonde hair that was put into a French twist at the back of her head. The style emphasized her slender throat, highlighting her distinctly Nordic-Teutonic facial features and put the enormous diamonds she had in her earlobes on full display. She paused just a moment and surveyed the tables at the outdoor café, and for a moment her ice blue eyes seemed to take in Boris, her gaze lingering with his for several seconds.

My God, she's stunning. Boris hoped like hell that the blonde angel had the heart of a devil and the soul and spirit of a slut.

A waitress approached her, and the two women exchanged words, but they were too softly spoken for Boris to hear them. Then, to Boris's limitless joy, the goddess was escorted to a table not far from his.

Boris tried to tell himself to not stare at the woman, but this was almost impossible when she crossed those endless legs at the knee and her black miniskirt pulled up even higher on her thighs. Almost all of her legs were exposed to Boris's greedy gaze.

She's the one I've been waiting for. He had the certainty of a man who had just become a True Believer.

Suddenly, a truly abhorrent thought crossed Boris's mind, and it hit him with such force that he flinched, almost as though he'd been struck by an invisible fist.

What if she's not alone? What if she's waiting for a man?

The possibility was too hideous for him to think about for more than a couple seconds. The Fates simply couldn't be that cruel, that sadistic. They wouldn't tempt and tease him like this, then snatch her away before he had even half a chance of winning her over and getting her back to the penthouse suite that cost him a small fortune and impressed every woman who saw it.

"Boss, over there," Arkady said, leaning to the side in his chair to get closer, and keeping his voice very low. "The big man in the black suit. See him?"

Boris was not inclined to look anywhere but in the direction of the blonde, but after several seconds he relented to his top bodyguard's wishes. He saw the man and sized him up as athletic, judging by his physique, and wealthy, judging by the quality of his clothes. Other than that, he saw nothing to interest him.

"So?" Boris said finally, turning his attention back to the blonde goddess who was sipping a martini. Boris was quite certain that he'd never seen such a kissable mouth in all his life.

"He was at the hotel the other day, and I think he was at the other hotel with us the night before that," Arkady said. "There's something about him that just isn't right."

Boris felt an immediate ice pick of apprehension stab him in the stomach. He had learned that when Arkady didn't like a situation, or a specific someone, there was probably a good reason for it.

"You think he followed us here?"

Arkady shook his head. "If he had tailed us, I would have

spotted it. No. It's something else, but I'm telling you now, his being here isn't a coincidence."

"I don't like coincidences. I don't believe in them." Boris took a sip of his drink to give himself a couple extra seconds to think about what his next move should be. "I want you to pick him up and question him. Find out if he's up to any-thing . . . then kill him. Understood?"

"Understood. Let me explain things to Vasily and Joseph, then you and I will take a little walk. I don't want you around when we take him away."

Boris turned his attention back to the woman and was pleased when she looked directly at him, then gave him a cryptic half-smile. She did not look away.

"Come on, Boss," Arkady said, his tone quiet but tense. "We've got to get you out of here." He stood quickly. "Let me take care of everything. I know just what to do."

Svetlana forced herself to appear calm, even if the emotions going through her were anything but calm. She had been sit-ting by herself, occasionally fending off businessmen who wanted to join her, when she saw Boris and his men step into the hotel's outdoor café. With any luck, she would at last come face-to-face with Boris, and her mission to put an end to his evil ways could progress to the next phase.

She had to get him away from his bodyguards. They were a hawk-eyed trio of killers. She had sized them up at first glance. She'd seen their type many times before, and on more than a few occasions had had to deal with such professionals.

She watched as Boris and one of his bodyguards rose from the table. The bodyguard was speaking in hushed tones di-rectly into Boris's ear for a moment, then Boris started walk-ing toward the door leading to the hotel's main lobby. As he walked, he looked at Svetlana and gave her a slight smile, one that was more than merely friendly, but not openly flirtatious.

She returned the smile with similar warmth.

He doesn't even go to the bathroom without taking a bodyguard with him.

She sipped her ice cold vodka martini and fought against the urge to turn in her chair to watch Boris step into the hotel's interior.

To begin with, when he comes back, I'll play it cool. Then I'll let him know with body language and eye signals that I'd like another martini, and a handsome man to share it with. That should break the ice and get this assignment moving in the right direction.

Svetlana could feel her confidence rising. The art of seduction? Flirting? She had earned her Ph.D. Magna Cum Lauda in eroticism. That was where she had home field advantage. That was where the war was being waged under circumstances that favored her. This kind of war was what she had been trained for. This was the reason Omega Force was created and had selected her years ago, when she was still in boot camp and so very young.

She watched as the remaining two bodyguards rose from their chairs, and she noticed that they looked to their left while trying to pretend that they *weren't* looking to their left. She followed their gaze, and it led to a big, remarkably handsome blond man with wide shoulders and clothes that suggested wealth. But there was something about the way he wore his fine clothes that whispered of a certain uncomfortableness with them. He hadn't grown up in wealth, Svetlana suspected. Money had come to him later in life, perhaps not until his adult years. He might even secretly harbor feelings of guilt over the vast profits that now came his way.

In the Ukraine, there were some people who now had more money than Midas, and this was a very new phenomenon.

But money didn't always buy happiness. He was staring rather morosely at the cocktail on his table.

Svetlana watched as the two bodyguards walked toward the hotel. They walked very slowly, as though they were taking their time, not only not in any hurry to leave, but not really wanting to leave. They stepped past the big man.

The sound of a car coming to a quick stop drew Svetlana's attention. She was less than thirty feet from the street and the sound of tires protesting against concrete that needed repairs startled her. The car was a big, black sedan, made by a German company. And through the open window of the right rear door she recognized the bodyguard who had escorted Boris out of the outdoor bar.

She turned her head just in time to watch as the bodyguards moved in on the big man. One of the men pulled a gun out of his suitcoat from beneath his left arm as the other one grabbed the big man by the wrist.

Kidnapping!

Svetlana had read several news accounts of how common it was in developing countries for wealthy young heirs to get kidnapped, and then be ransomed for a fortune back to their parents. She didn't know who the big man was, but he certainly didn't deserve whatever would befall him should he become a captive of Boris and his men.

As the criminals started pushing their captive toward the sedan, already getting him through the gate, Svetlana reached into her jacket pocket and grabbed the mother-of-pearl grips of her small Browning automatic.

"Stop!" she shouted, rising and thumbing off the safety of her weapon. She always kept a bullet in the chamber.

The gangster with the gun turned to aim at Svetlana. They were fifteen feet from each other when Svetlana squeezed the trigger.

The little gun barked and jumped in her hand—and she missed. Her bullet merely tugged at the gunman's coat as it slipped harmlessly between his ribs and elbow.

Cursing herself for being a poor marksman—how many times had Burke told her that she should put in some serious time at a gun range—Svetlana found herself looking down the muzzle of the gunman's pistol.

The big man in the black suit made his move, chopping down hard with his free hand on the forearm of the gunman. The pistol went off with an enormous roar that was deafening to the ears. It was a dozen times louder than Svetlana's little .25. The big man who had been taken captive let out a cry of agony and fell to the concrete sidewalk.

Svetlana squeezed the trigger a second time. This time her aim was true. A red spot, no bigger in circumference than that of a pencil, show on his white shirtfront, directly over his heart. His mouth opened, and in his eyes there was a look of astonished disbelief.

The other bodyguard was pulling a big pistol from his jacket. Svetlana adjusted her aim and squeezed the trigger. The man's head snapped back on his shoulders briefly, then he straightened himself and looked at Svetlana. There was a bullet hole in his face, just to the left of his nose. He started to raise his pistol, but now his movements were forced, the gun suddenly appearing very heavy.

Svetlana squeezed the trigger again, this time putting a bullet through his chest. Both he and his partner in crime fell at the same time, first to their knees, then onto their faces. Their corpses didn't even twitch.

The big man on the ground was clutching his leg, squeezing his thigh very near his crotch, as though to apply a tourniquet.

Svetlana turned her attention to the sedan, toward the one kidnapper who remained. But he was no longer an adversary. Her first shot — the one that she had thought had harmlessly missed its mark, leaving her target unscathed — had found another purpose. The man behind the steering wheel was now slumped over it, with blood dribbling down the side of his face. There was a bullet hole in his right temple. His eyes were still open.

"Come on," Svetlana said in Russian-accented English. "We've got to get you out of here."

"Yes," the big wounded man said in English, with the neutral accent of Middle America. "I . . . I think I can walk." Blood was pouring out of him from the bullet wound high on his left thigh, though this was hardly visible on his black trousers. "With help."

"Lean on me. We've got to get away from here," Svetlana said, taking his left arm by the wrist and sliding under it so that his arm was over her shoulders.

That was when she felt the big gun in the shoulder holster beneath his silk suit coat, and she realized that all of her perceptions and initial assumptions about what had just happened might have been completely, irretrievably, horrendously wrong.

Incongruously, beside the four-star hotel was a butcher shop, and above it were three floors of small apartments. Between the two buildings was an alley that was very narrow and looked as though it had been used as a garbage dump for some time and only occasionally cleaned. Svetlana headed for the alley, squeezing the wounded man tightly to her side, desperately needing to get away from the congested foot traffic of the main city streets.

"Do you have any place to stay?" she asked.

The man groaned, but did not answer. It didn't matter. Whatever he said would mean nothing, since the people who had tried to take him captive must surely know where he was lodging, so she'd have to find someplace else for him. Svetlana could see no option but to take him back to her hotel. It was three blocks away, and she wasn't at all certain he could make it that far. Now that he wasn't clutching his leg, the blood was pumping out of him even faster.

Burke's going to kill me for this. He hates it whenever I deviate from the mission.

In front of her were two drunks who were passing a bottle

of wine back and forth between them. At first they didn't see Svetlana and the wounded man, but when they did, they spread out slightly. They were intoxicated, but there was still a feral gleam in their eyes.

Svetlana reached into her pocket, extracted the little Browning automatic, and aimed it at the nearest man.

In Russian, she said, "Fuck with me and I'll kill you both."

They were drunk, but they weren't suicidal. Both men stepped aside, giving Svetlana plenty of room to walk between them.

To the wounded man she said, "What's your name?"

"It doesn't matter," he said, his voice hoarse as he limped along. "Why are you helping me? Who are you?"

"That's another thing that really doesn't matter right now. We've got to get you off the streets. I've got a hotel a couple blocks from here. With any luck we can get you in my room without the authorities being notified."

The wounded man stumbled twice on the way to the hotel, but he impressed Svetlana with his warrior's spirit. As they approached her hotel, they started drawing attention from pedestrians, so Svetlana began speaking in Russian-accented English.

"Why do you always have to drink so much? We were going to have such a good night, and now you've ruined it by sucking on a bottle of whiskey like it was my tits."

People around them started to laugh condescendingly, and she knew that she had taken the right approach to getting the big bleeding man out of the public and into her room.

When she stepped into the lobby of her hotel, which boasted of having the best accommodations in all of Kiev, several liveried bellmen started moving toward her, looks of concern on their faces. Svetlana immediately waved them away.

"He started drinking at noon," she said, slurring her words as though she, too, had been drinking for hours. "And now look at him. We were going to have such a wonderful night. Now he can hard walk, much less fuck." She groaned, making her way toward the elevator.

The wounded man was putting more weight on her with each step. Svetlana could tell that he didn't have much stamina left in him, no matter how great his warrior's heart. Two liveried bell boys started toward her again, but she waved them off angrily with her free hand.

"He's my problem, not yours," she said sharply, though she did not raise her voice.

The elevator seemed to take forever to arrive, though Svetlana knew that it was really only a minute, or perhaps a few seconds more. She got him inside, and when the doors closed, she punched the button for her sixth-floor suite.

"It won't be long now," she said to the man, speaking English, though she kept up her Russian accent. "Be strong for just a little bit longer. We've got to get that bleeding stopped, and then the healing can begin."

To her profound relief, there was no one in the hallway as she very nearly dragged the wounded man to her room. She was grateful that the nearly hundred-year-old hotel did not have any security cameras, like all the luxury hotels in America did. If she needed to make up a story, it would be so much easier without video surveillance proving she was lying.

From her purse she extracted the magnetic key card, stuffed it into the door lock, and staggered inside. By this time Svetlana had to support nearly all of the big man's weight. She practically dragged him to her king-sized bed, then tossed him onto it.

She immediately began administering what little medical skills she possessed, hoping like hell that the big man wouldn't die in her room. Corpses had a tendency to draw the attention of men Svetlana wasn't interested in meeting.

Burke's going to be so pissed at me. He told me from the very beginning to mind my own business and to never take in strays.

Dmitri was only partially conscious, but he was aware of the fact that he was dying. The gun had been a .45, one of the most lethal calibers in the world. When he had karate-chopped the gunman's arm, Dmitri had lost balance slightly, so he couldn't quite put all the strength he wanted to behind the attack. When the gun went off, it sent a semi-jacketed hollow-point into Dmitri's thigh. But instead of hitting him solidly so that the bullet would go in the front of his leg and out the back of it, it took a path that tore along the inside of his leg, but in doing so, caused much more tissue damage.

Hitting the inside of Dmitri's thigh, the slug instantly mushroomed and ripped a furrow in his flesh an inch wide and nearly three inches long. Though the bullet had missed Dmitri's femoral artery, it had blasted out an enormous amount of skin and muscle.

Dmitri blinked his eyes several times in an attempt to focus his vision. After several seconds, the haze receded, and he could see clearly. He watched as the woman put a common sewing needle in one side of the wound, then into the other, then ease the thread through. She was slowly and methodically stitching close his wound.

Where in hell did she get needle and thread? Dmitri tried to focus his thoughts, and found that he couldn't.

When she reached the end of the bloody valley in his thigh, she began sewing back toward where she started, pinching the wound closed with her left hand as she used her right to finesse the needle and thread through the skin. When Dmitri realized that he hadn't remembered when she had begun closing his wound, he knew that he must have previously lost consciousness. He wondered how long he had been out, and how long he had to live.

What did he remember? He remembered being in the hotel

lobby, and the woman pretending that she had been drinking, and telling the bellboys that he had been drinking since noon. Dmitri remembered the elevator doors closing behind them after they'd stepped in, but he couldn't remember them opening again, or his walking into her room. Had she carried him?

As he watched the woman slowly sewing closed his wound, he thought about the mission he had been sent on by General Lebedev, and how it had gone so terribly wrong.

He hadn't been betrayed. Of that Dmitri was certain. The fact that Boris's men had known he was a threat could only meant that Dmitri had slipped up somewhere. He suspected he had been spotted during his reconnaissance but hadn't realized it. That mistake had very nearly cost him his life. As he thought about his mistake, wondering just exactly when he had been spotted, it occurred to him that he might still lose his life.

How much blood could a man lose before life slips away? Two pints? Maybe three, at most?

In his semi-conscious state, an emotion went through Dmitri that was unusual for him. He felt embarrassment that was so acute it bordered on shame.

I fucked up.

The awareness of his own mistake was like acid in his stomach. It was eating him up from the inside.

I thought I was so goddamned clever, but they spotted me, so now I've got some woman I don't know trying her best to keep me from bleeding to death. Damn. Goddamn. All these years in the field, and I make a dumb-assed mistake like that!

He closed his eyes, and though he tried to will himself into staying awake, his eyes refused to open, and his breathing became slow, shallow, and even.

CHAPTER FIVE

That's a big cock.
The thought made Svetlana squeeze her eyes tightly shut
for just a moment as guilt washed over her. She turned her
gaze up to the man's face and felt a certain sense of relief that
he wasn't looking at her. His eyes were closed, and he seemed
to be sleeping.

She set the needle down on his thigh, then reached up and
touched his neck. His pulse was even, but weak. He'd lost a
lot of blood, and though he was a big and healthy man, there
had to be limits to his strength and endurance. Every man had
limits. Svetlana suspected that he hadn't emptied the deep
well of his reserves, but she was certain that it would take him
days to recover.

It's just a flesh wound. Svetlana tried to tell herself that,
though even she didn't believe it inconsequential. Mere flesh
wounds had killed countless gunshot victims, and Svetlana
knew it, though she was trying to believe otherwise.

Svetlana eased the needle through the man's skin one more
time, then decided that she had stitched closed his wound as
best she could. She tied off the thread.

Now what the hell do I do? Svetlana was thinking that in all
her years with Omega Force, she'd never made such a stupid
mistake as to get involved in a fight that didn't involve either
her or her country.

Something was wrong. The general could feel it in the

marrow of his bones. A soldier like Dmitri didn't simply not report in unless there was a very good reason, and General Lebedev had already made it quite clear that there was never a very good reason for not keeping in contact when on assignment.

So what the hell had gone wrong? Any of a thousand things, the general knew. The Red Star Unit was operating with official but unacknowledged authorization, and that was the reason its soldiers nearly always worked entirely alone. If they got caught during the course of their assignment, then they would be disavowed. Superior officers would say they were shocked, and there would be the cliché excuse of a soldier having gone rogue.

And since the government owned the media, there wouldn't be a lot of investigating, and if there was, the conclusions would be decided in the Kremlin, and long before the so-called investigators had finished writing their report. End of story.

The Kremlin always had the final say in such matters.

He was hearing rumbling and rumors from his spies in Kiev. Something had happened. What, exactly, that *something* was had yet to be determined. But the Kiev police had gotten involved, and they were asking questions.

The general's contempt for Ukraine escalated just a little bit in his soul. Since the breakup of the Soviet Union, he had hated Ukraine above all the other countries that had once been an integral part of the greater nation. But he hated Ukraine more than the others. More even than Latvia. Much more than the Czech Republic, toward which he harbored some gentle feelings, since his grandmother had been born there and was now buried there.

So what the hell had Dmitri gotten himself up to?

He had stopped bleeding. Svetlana had stared at the sutured wound, virtually without blinking, for several minutes. It wasn't until she was absolutely convinced that the bleeding had stopped that she took off the top sheet of the bed and tore it into wide, long strips to make bandages. With the gentle touch that mothers use for their children, she bandaged the big man's wound.

It wasn't until she had finished wrapping the cotton around the damaged leg that she finally closed her eyes, breathed a sigh of relief, and told herself that if ever there was a time in her life when she deserved to have a cocktail, it was here and now.

Svetlana looked at the big man and made sure that he was sleeping. Then she shrugged off her suit coat and tossed it into a chair. After only a moment of deliberation, she unbuttoned her blouse and removed it, tossing it on top of her coat. She unzipped her skirt and slithered out of it, tossing it onto the other garments. She deliberated for a moment, then reached behind her back and unhooked her brassiere. It, too, went on top of her heap of discarded clothing. Being braless, she sighed with contentment. Though it was still early evening, she felt like she had been awake for days.

Clothed now in only bikini panties, she picked up a lowball glass, then went to the small refrigerator so common in all fine hotels throughout the world. Inside she found a small tray of ice cubes in the tiny freezer — if she wanted more, she'd have to get them from the ice machine down the hall — and a small plastic bottle of vodka. She noted that though there were several different brands of vodka, none of them were distilled in Russia.

This didn't surprise her. She selected a Swedish brand of vodka that had always pleased her. After filling her lowball glass with ice, she poured the small plastic bottle of vodka into the glass, and then a second one. Satisfied with her libation, she sat down in an overstuffed chair, looked out at the sun as it set on the city of Kiev, and tried to figure out what in hell she was going to do next.

Since the authorities hadn't kicked in her door or even knocked on it, Svetlana knew that—at least in the short term—she had made a successful getaway after killing Boris's three bodyguards.

She finished her cocktail and thought about what moves to make next. Judging by how pale the big man was, it would take him at least a couple days before he could travel. That wasn't necessarily a bad thing. After an incident like the one she'd just been in, the authorities would be keeping a vigilant eye on all the modes of transportation out of the city, especially the airport. Best to lay low for now and give the police time to assume that a successful escape from the city had been affected.

She picked up the man's trousers, which she had taken off him with his help before he closed his eyes and unconsciousness claimed him. The trousers were heavy with blood, and when Svetlana got some on her right hand, she grimaced.

You'd think that someone in my line of work wouldn't be so squeamish about blood. She wiped her fingers clean on a white towel that was already stained with blood.

She found his wallet in the back right pocket. He had a driver's license issued from the State of Nebraska in the United States, as well as some Ukrainian hryvnia, and less than a hundred dollars in American currency. She looked at the plastic driver's license. It said his name was David Klein.

The Beretta with the silencer informed her that his name really wasn't David Klein.

From her luggage she removed an Omega Force-issued electronic tablet and touched the power button. When the computer had powered up, she placed the pad of her right thumb on the middle of the glass screen. After several seconds, a slender green bar of light formed on the screen, then made its way slowly down Svetlana's thumb, then disappeared.

Svetlana waited several seconds, then placed her entire hand on the screen. Several more seconds passed before the green bar of light appeared again, this time running the entire width of the screen. The light went slowly over Svetlana's palm. The screen went blank, and when it reappeared, there was the image of a computer keyboard.

Using her index fingers, Svetlana typed, "Who is this man? I need to know ASAP."

Walking over to the bed, she used the tablet to take several pictures of the big man's face. Then one of his driver's license.

She touched the button that read "SEND" and the screen went blank once again.

Svetlana set the tablet down on the desk, then sat in the chair and thought about what to do next.

She'd have to contact the hotel, first things first. She was booked only until the following morning, then the hotel expected her to leave. That had to change, because the big man wouldn't be in any condition to walk. Should it be known that he was wounded, hotel management would undoubtedly contact the police, and then they would find out for themselves *why* he was wounded. The situation would get really bad after that.

An idea came to Svetlana, and she smiled. She drank the last of the vodka as she swirled ice cubes around in the lowball glass.

She picked up the telephone and got room service.

"We'll need a bottle of whiskey and a bottle of vodka, and a bottle of vermouth. We'll need a bottle of stuffed olives. And a bucket of ice. No, better make that two buckets of ice." She looked at the big man sleeping naked on his back in her king-sized bed, then said into the telephone, "And send up half a dozen cold cut sandwiches. Ham and cheese. Maybe some salami or turkey. That sort of thing. Make sure the bread is perfection. He's worked up quite an appetite." Svetlana giggled as though she'd just been touched intimately. "Give me just a moment, and then you can touch me wherever you want," she said teasingly, pretending to be talking to her lover. "Better send up caviar for two, along with thin toast for it."

Closing the connection, Svetlana went to the bed and then very slowly, very gently, eased the man from his back onto his stomach. She turned his face away from the door, then adjusted the bed spread so that it covered his bandaged left leg, but nothing else about him. She moved a pillow so that his face couldn't be seen.

She went to the mini-refrigerator and extracted all the whiskey bottles inside. Moving quickly now, since room service was always fast for anyone in the luxury rooms no matter what the country was, she unscrewed the caps of the bottles, then dumped the contents in various places on the carpeting around the room. With the last two bottles, she poured half the contents in her mouth, swished it around with her tongue, then spit it onto the carpeting. She poured half the contents of a bottle into her left palm, then rubbed the whiskey into her right breast and stomach. She emptied the plastic bottle into her right palm, and repeated the process. She, and the room, now reeked of whiskey.

The soft knock at the door came just as Svetlana was finishing making her room ready for inspection. She unfastened the chain lock on the door, then opened it just enough to stick her face between the door and frame. The bellboy looked to be in his late fifties or early sixties, and he had in front of him a wheeled cart with all the items that Svetlana had requested.

"Oh . . . oh, dear," Svetlana said, slurring her English words. "You'll need a tip, won't you? I hadn't thought that far ahead, I guess." She nibbled on her lower lip for a moment, and saw the libidinous appreciation come to light in the old man's eyes. "Promise you won't tell anyone what you see?"

In English, but with a Ukrainian accent—Svetlana had no doubt that the night manager had informed him as to what language to speak—the bellboy said, "In all my years at this hotel, I've never seen anything, Miss Simonov." He put a hand over his heart to add sincerity to the proclamation.

He knows my name. Management has been talking about me.

"Bring it in, please," she said, opening the door wide as she crossed her left arm over her naked breasts. "Near the desk, if you would be so kind."

The big man was on his stomach, completely naked, with only his left leg hidden by the bed spread. The bellboy glanced at him, but did no more than that. Then he turned his back to the bed and faced Svetlana. His expression was poker-blank, but Svetlana suspected his emotions weren't so blasé.

She went to the desk where she'd placed the man's wallet, then gave the bellboy an embarrassed, guilty look before using both hands—and therefore putting her naked breasts on display—to open the wallet. She thumbed through the paper money slowly, giving the old man a good view of what he would undoubtedly be talking about later.

"Thank you so much," Svetlana said, finally extracting the one currency that had real value the world over. She held an American twenty dollar bill in her hand. "I'm sure I'll be calling you again soon. You know how Americans are. They love their whiskey more than they love their mothers."

"Yes, Miss Simonov. My name is Josef. If you would be so kind, should ever you need anything, please ask for me personally."

"Of course, my charming man. Of course!"

When she was alone with the wounded man, Svetlana went to the bathroom and used soap and a washcloth to clean off the whiskey she'd doused herself with. She went to the cart, lifted the silver dome off the round tray beneath, and found ten sandwiches made with an assorted meats and cheeses. She decided that decent food would be better for her right then than caviar and champagne.

So, now I've got a cover story on why I'm staying extra days at the hotel, but I've still got to figure out how to get out of Kiev.

In less that fifteen minutes after she had requested information from Omega Force via her electronic tablet, she heard the soft chime, and knew that she'd received a response. She went through the scanning routine with thumb and palm, then stepped into the bathroom and closed and locked the door.

After she tapped the proper keys, the image of a handsome young man in a Russian military uniform came on the screen. He was wearing his hat, as all soldiers did for their formal portraits. He looked at least a decade younger than he did now.

She tapped several more keys, and the information on the young soldier began scrolling from bottom upward on the screen. Svetlana, impatient to know who the big, naked stranger was in her bed, decided she would skim the information presented to her to begin with, then go back to the beginning and give it all a thorough reading.

His real name was Major Dmitri Kuzetsov, and he was now thirty-four years old . . . he wasn't married and never had been . . . he was a member of the GRU, the Russian version of the Central Intelligence Agency . . . his area of expertise was satellite photo analysis . . .

Bullshit. They don't give their satellite photo geeks Berettas equipped with silencers.

She continued reading, but with much less interest now that she was certain what was written was for consumption by foreign intelligence agencies. Admitting that Dmitri — and the name fit him a lot better than David, Svetlana decided, because there some something exotic and erotic about it — worked for the GRU gave him a solid alibi for going to the intelligence agency's headquarters in Moscow every day. She'd seen the building several times, but only from across the street. It was a massive building, and there were thousands of men and women who worked there every day. And though some of them were no doubt most closely associated with the nefarious activities of the old KGB, the vast majority of them were exactly what Dmitri's cover said he was — an analyst. Just one of a legion of clever young men and women who stared intently all day at a computer screen, trying to figure out what the other side was up to.

It was the same at CIA headquarters in Langley, Virginia. Scores and scores of geeks, with only a few spies, agents, and assassins thrown into the mix just in case the world got interesting.

A myriad of mixed emotions went through Svetlana as she stood in the bathroom trying to figure out what her next move should be. If Dmitri really was who his file said he was — or at least some watered-down version of it — then he was likely an enemy of Omega Force, and of the United States. Yet Svetlana had saved his life, and she'd even killed three men doing it. And now she was harboring him, keeping him safe from Boris, and from the Ukrainian authorities, who no doubt wanted to know who the hell had caused all the commotion on the streets of Kiev. Even in Ukraine, the authorities took a very dim view of that kind of gunplay. After all, Svetlana reasoned, Kiev wasn't New Orleans, Chicago, or even Baltimore.

She read Dmitri's dossier one more time, this time slowly and carefully, word for word. She couldn't find any slip-ups by whoever had created his cover. No inadvertent clues that the big, muscular man named Dmitri was anything other than a man who studied satellite photographs of opposition troop and artillery movements, then tried to figure out what those movements meant.

Svetlana thought briefly of putting a word in to Burke to get his advice on what she should do next. She almost instantly discarded this idea. She had already contacted him once, which meant that there was the possibility — however remote — that the signal could have been intercepted. The whole concept of Omega Force was predicated on the fact that agents didn't know who they worked for other than their immediate superior. Svetlana knew Burke. She didn't know who or what he knew. If she was captured, all she could give her captors was a name, which she knew was an alias.

So, now that you know David is really Dmitri, what are you going to do about it? Svetlana closed her eyes for a moment as she squeezed the bathroom doorknob. *I guess I'm playing this assignment by the seat of my pants.*

This was not the way she liked her assignments to play out.

The stench of whiskey — stale whiskey at that, which was so much worse than fresh whiskey — assaulted Dmitri's olfactory senses the instant he reached full consciousness. Without moving a muscle, or even blinking his eyes, he reconstructed his world just the way it had been before he had lost consciousness.

Oh, yes, there was that woman — that very, very special woman, and she had been sewing closed the rip in his thigh that looked more like a fleshy valley of oozing red meat and blood than a bullet wound.

A fucking .45. Why do the least talented among us always use hand-cannons instead of something civilized, something a bit more professional?

He knew the reason for that. When you don't know for certain precisely where your bullet is going to strike a body, better to use a really big damn bullet and make up for lack of skill with raw, brute force.

He felt the throbbing in his leg, and hoped like hell that beneath the makeshift bandage the skin wasn't turning pink with infection. As long as the wound didn't get infected, he would eventually recover his strength. But getting an infection was a real game changer. That was when the odds of escape immediately went from being in his favor to him being the odds-on-favorite to get a bullet in the back of the head from the Ukrainian Secret Service.

He heard soft, shallow breathing beside him. This wasn't the first time since the gunfight that he'd woken to find her sleeping. He suspected that she had stayed awake when he was unconscious so that she could tend to his wound, should there be anything more that she could do. He reflected that she had already done so much for him. He couldn't think of asking her to do anything more.

He moved his upper body just enough to pick up his cell phone from the bedside table. He tapped in the numbers to access a secure line to HQ, waited several seconds for the next prompt, thumbed more numbers in, then turned the phone in his hand and took several photographs of the sleeping woman. He touched a button on the phone's side, and the photographs disappeared.

As he waited for a response from his Red Star Unit comrades, he let his gaze roam slowly over the blonde woman. She was wearing a pale silk nightgown that was delicately embroidered. He hoped he'd soon know her identity.

What did he already know about her? That she was tall and shapely and beautiful? One look at her told him that. But what else did he know? For one thing, she was a crack marksman, even with a tiny mouse pistol that was more a gold-plated piece of art or jewelry than an assassin's weapon. Another thing about her was that she was no stranger to being smack dab in the middle of a gunfight. She had known instantly that the getaway driver behind the steering wheel was the man she had to kill first. Only then could she turn her attention to the other two, even though they were closer. Had she taken out the closest man first, the driver could have stomped on the accelerator and made a hasty exit from the bloody scene, or had time to draw a gun and enter the fray.

A gunfighter only learned skills like that by having honed them with real-world experience. Dmitri had been in too many battles to not recognize a professional when he saw one.

The phone vibrated in his hand, and Dmitri thumbed in the appropriate numbers. Within seconds he was looking at various photographs of a woman he now knew was named Svetlana Simonov, who was twenty-eight—and something of an enigma. It seemed that neither the GRU nor anyone else knew anything about her until ten years earlier, when she suddenly started jet-setting around the world with a fistful of credit cards that paid for a lifestyle that was lavish in the extreme. Nobody knew anything about her early life, but the big brains at the Red Star Unit did speculate that she had probably been attending a private school in Europe somewhere, living under an assumed name until she graduated and came of age.

Dmitri looked from his phone over to the sleeping woman. She was under the bedspread. He suspected the bedspread was hiding shapely legs and a pair of bikini panties. The last time he'd woken to find her in bed with him, she had been wearing panties. For the first time in his adult life, Dmitri was near a woman wearing scant lingerie, and he had no intentions of trying to seduce her.

He read a few more sections of the report, found that virtually every "fact" that Red Star could give him was really either informed speculation or a flat-out guesswork. Then the woman—Dmitri reminded himself that he could think of her as Svetlana, but he mustn't say her name aloud—made a soft groan, blinked her eyes several times, then looked at the phone in his hand. After several seconds, she looked at him and smiled.

"How are you feeling?" she asked, her Russian accent a little thicker and a bit muzzy with sleep.

He found her voice very pleasing to the senses.

"Hungry," he said in English. "Hungry and thirsty."

"That's a good sign. It means you're healing." She tossed the bedspread aside and slipped her legs athletically over the side of the mattress. Her breasts moved freely, unhindered beneath the thin silk.

"I got food and drink ordered for you." She put her hands on her shapely hips and looked down as Dmitri remained reclining in bed. "Can I call you Dmitri and speak Russian, or do you want to keep up this charade?"

He tried to come up with a lie, but couldn't think of one that was even remotely believable.

"I did a facial recognition background check on you, and since you've got your phone in hand, I suspect you've just done the same with me."

Dmitri gave her a crooked smile.

"Svetlana. That's a pretty name," he said, speaking Russian. "It seems you're quite a mystery to the people I work for."

"You mean the GRU?" she asked, also speaking Russian. "When did they start issuing pistols with silencers to satellite photo analysts?"

"That's a recent departmental change in policy," Dmitri said, now openly grinning.

CHAPTER SIX

Paris, France

Boris walked through the jetway and into Paris-Charles de Gaulle Airport, his heart pounding and his palms clammy as he carried his suitcase in one hand and his computer bag in the other. He knew that if the authorities were going to pounce, they'd do it here, in the airport, not wait until he was outside.

He saw uniformed French soldiers carrying short, fully automatic weapons. All of them were young, cold-eyed, physically fit. They were also ready, willing, and able to kill if that was what they had to do to keep the innocent tourists in Paris safe. In many ways, tourists were the lifeblood of France — most especially Paris.

Several of the young soldiers gave him the visual once-over, but none did more than that. He appeared to be just one of hundreds of middle-aged businessmen dragging along his suitcase full of clothes and his computer, returning home from a working trip to Eastern Europe.

As he walked nearer to the glass doors leading to a large stand of taxicabs, Boris breathed the first easy breath he'd taken since he discovered, days earlier, that the three men he had paid good money to every week to keep him safe had all been executed. He didn't know who had done the killing, but he was certain that he was the real target, not his bodyguards. With that knowledge secure in his brain, he decided immediately that any city in the world would be safer for him than

Kiev.

Paris is the unofficial mercenary capital of the world. I have friends here. I know people — the right kind of people to help me out at a time like this.

A middle-aged woman wearing a high visibility reflector vest to indicate she worked for the airport hailed a taxicab for him. Boris thanked her and palmed her some money, under-tipping slightly, as a man would when he's been on the road and he's spent more money while away from his wife than he should.

The taxi driver was dark-skinned, in his middle-twenties. Boris guessed that he'd come from North Africa. Somalia? Morocco? There were a lot of young men who looked like that in Paris these days, Boris thought. He hated every one of them.

In very serviceable French, Boris gave him the name of the hotel he knew he was welcome at. He'd stayed there several times before, and there had never been any trouble. Also, the bar at the hotel often had professional and semi-professional women plying their trade. Having his bodyguards shot and killed had disrupted every aspect of his life, both professional and romantic. He'd gone much longer than he wanted without either closing a deal or enjoying hot sex.

In the back seat of the Japanese-made sedan, Boris closed his eyes and plotted out his next moves. Step One was to get three trained mercenaries to guard him. Step Two was to find at least one woman he could fuck hard, then discard. Step Three was to start making phone calls to reestablish himself on the international contraband stage. Step Four was to get in touch with one of his banks — he was thinking of the one in the Bahamas — to get a steady flow of cash.

Now he was confident in what he was doing, and he felt good about that. Her didn't like uncertainty, and he most as-suredly didn't like chaos. Since learning that Arkady, Vasily, and Joseph had all been assassinated, he'd found his carefully orchestrated life had been thrown into utter disarray.

But that was all behind him. Now he was in Paris, a city he knew well.

The wound itched like hell, but there was no infection, and it had been days now since that big-bore bullet had blown a thumb-shaped furrow in his left thigh. He took the bottle of rubbing alcohol and a cotton ball, saturated the cotton, then dabbed the liquid onto his sutured wound. There was some stinging as the alcohol did its work, but not nearly as much as there had been days earlier.

After cleansing the wound thoroughly – it was the second time that day that he'd performed the procedure – he took a long strip of clean bandage, made from the top bed sheet, then slowly began winding it around his leg.

There was a light rap of knuckles on the door. Three quick knocks, one long one, and then three more quick ones. That meant that Svetlana had returned and there was no danger. His nine millimeter pistol with the silencer was on the bedside table, easily within reach, should her knock have been anything other than what it was.

She came into the room wearing a smile that Dmitri had learned to love. She also wore a navy blue mini dress that showed off those glorious legs of hers and something more than just a hint of cleavage.

So far, Dmitri had kept his hands to himself, but now that he was feeling so much better – Svetlana had been making sure that he was eating properly, and in all other ways being thoroughly pampered, nursed, and cared for – he was spending a lot less time worrying about his wound and the pain it caused him, and much more time thinking about Svetlana and the pleasure she might cause him.

"How are you?" Svetlana asked with sincerity, just as she

always did whenever she returned from an outing. She set down two plastic bags filled with new purchases and looked intently at him with piercing blue eyes.

"Ready to get home," Dmitri replied honestly. "I just disinfected the wound and put on a fresh bandage."

"What about the travel arrangements? I paid the hotel through tomorrow morning."

"We're leaving tonight, just as I'd promised we would." When her lips curled into a grateful, relieved smile, Dmitri thought that he'd very much like to find out for himself just exactly how delicious those lips were. "We're in the back of a commercial panel truck to get out of the city, then we transfer to a freight delivery van to cross the border into Belarus. There's a plane with twin turbo prop engines, and extra fuel capacity, to take us to Moscow."

She turned her back to him and began removing men's slacks and shirts from the plastic bags. She bent slightly at the waist, and her mini dress — which under even the most modest of circumstances, didn't cover much of her legs — pulled up slightly to show even the very tops of her thighs.

Dmitri wondered if she was wearing panties. Just asking himself the question was exciting.

Dmitri felt his cock stirring, and he tried to tell himself that it was a sign that he was healing nicely, but he knew that it was really only a symptom of being horny, and that Svetlana was very enticing to look at. Very.

Moscow, Russia

They landed at a small, private airport on the southern outskirts of Moscow. A large, French-made sedan with darkened windows was waiting for them. As the twin-engine plane taxied closer to the four buildings that constituted the entire airport, the driver's side door opened and a young man in military uniform got out. He was tall and slender, and moved with a certain feline grace that Svetlana had learned to associate with servicemen familiar with their craft.

The side door of the plane was opened, and the young soldier, with a nod to Dmitri but not a salute to acknowledge his status because he wasn't in uniform, said, "I'll get the luggage, sir. General Lebedev is waiting for you in the car."

Svetlana watched as Dmitri patted the young soldier on the shoulder. Now that they were in Russia, he seemed a much more gentle man, as though all the sharp edges to his soul had been smoothed with a delicate hand. She wondered what it would be like to relax with him, reading books together without talking while sipping a nice glass of chardonnay.

Easy, Svetlana. Letting your emotions go very far in that direction is a recipe for disaster.

The soldier helped Svetlana step down the short ladder from the plane to the tarmac. Though the pilot had idled the engines, there was still a strong wind when Svetlana was directly in the wake, and it blew her hair around untidily.

So much for making a good first impression. Svetlana was instantly annoyed. Dmitri had warned her that his direct superior officer would most assuredly meet them at the airport, so she knew what to expect.

As they approached the sedan, the rear door opened and a broad-shouldered man with a formidable mustache and a round, perfectly bald head stepped out. He was in the uniform of a general. Dmitri walked directly to him, stood at attention, then snapped off a brisk salute. The general smiled, saluted, then reached out a hand. The two men shook hands, and Svetlana could tell that though there was a significant difference in their rank, and in their age, there was a great deal of mutual respect.

The general looked at Svetlana, smiled, and said, "I like this woman already."

As the sedan made its way into the heart of the city, Dmitri and the general talked in quiet undertones, and Svetlana kept herself busy by looking at the sights of the city. She didn't enjoy Moscow as much as she did St. Petersburg, but in the last ten years — since she had started working for Omega Force — she had been to the heart of Mother Russia at least three or four times a year.

To Svetlana, Dmitri said, "We'll take you to your hotel where you can get comfortable and relax. I've got to go to the office. That'll take several hours."

"What hotel are you taking me to?" Svetlana asked. When Dmitri gave her the name, she shook her head with a bit more vehemence than she had intended, sending her blonde hair swirling around her shoulders, and made a waving motion with her hands. "I'd much rather stay at the Palace Hotel. They know me there, and they've got the best staff in all of Moscow. Probably the best in all of Russia. It's in Rublyovka."

"The lady knows her way around Russia," General Lebedev said, his smile broadening.

Svetlana looked at him, and with a twinkle in her blue eyes, replied, "The lady knows her way around the world."

Svetlana surprised and impressed Dmitri and the general when the day manager at the Palace Hotel recognized her the instant she walked through the front doors. He hurried around the front desk to greet her personally, and bowed very respectfully. When he looked at the general, his eyes took on a certain worried quality.

"Everything is all right, Victor," Svetlana said, taking the elderly man's hand in both of hers, and patting the back of it. "My life has been a little crazy lately, so I'm hoping that I can come here and do nothing more strenuous than relax."

"The Premiere Suite is available," the manager said, then after some hesitation, added, "for you."

Svetlana suspected that someone else had a reservation, and though they didn't know it yet, they had just *lost* that reservation for the Premiere Suite.

Paris, France

"And these men—you trust them?" Boris asked a mercenary named Oleg.

"I've worked with both of them before," the mercenary replied. He was in his late forties and had a long white scar that ran from his forehead, over his left eye, then down to his left cheek. "Mostly in Beirut, but also in Mogadishu."

Boris looked at the man, thinking that he wouldn't be nearly so ugly if he would wear an eye patch. His left eye seemed to have only the white left. There was no pupil in the eye whatsoever. It would be better to keep it hidden, Boris decided.

"I'll pay you, and you can pay them whatever you think is necessary. Agreed?"

"Agreed. Money in advance, one week at a time. Agreed?"

"Agreed," Boris replied. He knew the score and how business of this nature was supposed to be conducted. He didn't intend on staying in Paris more than six weeks, and that was all the longer he would need them. Then he'd move on.

"You realize, of course, that if she is in any way connected to the Russian Mafia, that I'll probably give you the assignment to kill her?" General Lebedev said, sitting behind his desk. Small puffs of cigarette smoke were expelled from his mouth and nostrils as he spoke.

"Yes, sir, I'm aware of that," Dmitri answered.

"Tell her nothing of the Red Star Unit. Or, at least, tell her as little as possible. If she can be an asset for us, then she has value. If she is a threat, then she must be neutralized." He sighed. "But, of course, she might be one of ours, and we're not getting through the cover we've concocted ourselves." He sighed again. "She might already be working for us, and we don't know it."

"Yes, sir. Of course. And that's as it should be." Understanding that the meeting was now over, Dmitri rose to his feet. He wanted to get to his two-bedroom apartment, shower and shave and put on a crisply laundered uniform, then return to Svetlana. In the short time that they'd been together, he'd learned to crave her companionship. "When do you want me on duty, sir?"

"Take two days off, then come in first thing in the morning. I should have some information on the whereabouts of Boris Antonich by then." He stubbed out his cigarette, then reached for the fresh red pack on his desk. He started removing the cellophane. "Your assignment isn't over until that bastard's dead and gone."

"Yes, sir," Dmitri said, feeling as though he had let his superior officer down terribly by not killing Boris. It was a feeling he seldom experienced, and one that he loathed with all his heart and soul.

I'm not a teenager going out on a date and about to meet my girl's father for the first time. Dmitri checked himself in the mirror in the hotel's elevator. *Well, of course she's in the most exclusive room in the hotel. What else would you expect of her?*

The elevator seemed to take forever to get to the top floor of the hotel. Reaching down, Dmitri scratched his bandaged wound through the trousers of his crisp brown dress uniform. The wound was healing nicely, and the doctor who had examined him said that whoever had put in the stitches had been "crude but effective." The doctor knew enough about the GRU to not ask too many questions about an obvious gunshot wound.

The elevator doors opened onto Svetlana's floor. Dmitri made a point of not limping as he stepped out of the elevator, oriented himself as to where he was and where Svetlana's room would be, then walked purposefully to her room. He rapped his knuckles on the door.

Several seconds ticked by. *Hurry up, damn it. Svetlana, what's taking you so long?* He gave his head a little shake. *Settle down, for Christ's sake.*

In a voice that teased, from inside the room Svetlana asked sweetly, "Who is it?"

Dmitri looked straight at the spyglass in the door and said with mock anger, "You know damned well who it is."

Fantastic. She's always in a good mood when she teases.

He heard the lock being removed and felt a sudden tightness in his stomach. He realized at that moment that he reacted differently to Svetlana than he did with other women. In his life, she was completely unique.

When the door opened, with crystalline clarity he understood why he reacted more powerfully to Svetlana than to any other woman he'd ever known.

She was wearing a long black nightgown. The silk was of the finest quality, the lace trimming hand stitched with skill and loving care. And though Dmitri wasn't an expert in such frivolous things, he suspected the lace was Italian in origin. The décolletage was so deeply veed that not only could he see the pale erotic inner swells of her jutting breasts, he could see her navel with the three-diamond jewelry in its piercing. Back in Kiev she had told him that the top diamond, which nestled in the hollow of her navel, was a three carat diamond, the second one, attached by a small gold chain to the first, was a two carat diamond, and the third in the string was one carat.

It occurred to him that most Russians worked their entire life without ever making enough money to pay for jewelry like that.

The nightgown came down to the floor in midnight black opulence. Peeking out beneath the bottom hem he saw her toes. Her nails were painted a brilliant red. Dmitri couldn't say why he suddenly found the sight of a woman's toes so erotic, he only knew that he did.

"Hello, Dmitri," Svetlana said, her voice warm and assured. "I'm so glad you've come to see me." She waited until Dmitri's gaze made its way slowly up her body and to her eyes before saying, "Won't you please come in? I've ordered some libations from room service that I think we'll enjoy."

She moved aside, and Dmitri stepped into the suite of rooms. A living room angled off to the right, with a large flat-screen TV, as well as library shelves filled with hardbound books. Hidden speakers played Vivaldi softly. To the left was a dining room table big enough to seat six, as well as a two-burner stove and a full-size refrigerator. He could only assume that, should he enter deeper into the suite, he'd find at least one luxurious bedroom, and probably two.

Off to the right, facing the living room, was a fireplace. It was gas, not wood, but it was extraordinarily realistic. Dmitri didn't realize it was gas until he was standing directly in front of it.

In the room, the only light came from a single lamp set near the long sofa, and the fireplace.

"I must say, you do know how to live in style," Dmitri said, with much less censure in his tone than he actually felt. He didn't make enough money in a month to pay for what this room would cost for a night.

"Go over there," she said, making a vague gesture with her hand toward the fireplace. "I'll make you something to drink. I've ordered a bottle of excellent Russian vodka. I know you like it straight, but do you want ice, or no?"

"With ice, please. But I'm not fussy."

The sexual tension was so thick in the air that Dmitri could practically taste it. Svetlana had turned and was walking toward the dining room table, where an assortment of liquor bottles and two large buckets of ice waited. He noted there was also a bottle of champagne in an ice-filled bucket, and that the bottle had been uncorked. He suspected the champagne was very exclusive. Svetlana didn't do things in half measures.

As Svetlana walked away, Dmitri's focus went from the long, streaky blonde hair cascading down her back and shoulders, to the twin swells of her bottom undulating beneath the sheer silk.

There are asses, and then there are perfect asses. Svetlana's definitely got a perfect ass.

She made a vodka on the rocks for him. He noted from the label that she had ordered one of the most expensive vodkas in the world.

She poured a glass of champagne for herself.

The breath caught in Dmitri's throat when Svetlana returned, walking slowly, only this time instead of her succulent bottom drawing his gaze like a magnet, it was the fullness of her heavy, firm breasts, wobbling erotically, pale against the raven-black silk décolletage.

"Here you go," she said, handing him a heavy crystal lowball glass. She raised her champagne flute. "To getting out of Kiev alive."

Dmitri clinked his glass against hers, shook his head in negation of her toast, and said in a low, deep voice, "To *us* for getting each other out of Kiev. I wouldn't have survived without you."

"If not for you I'd probably either be hiding in my room right now, or in police custody." She brought the glass to her lips and took a small sip, her gaze locked with Dmitri's. "We made a pretty good team."

"*Make* a pretty good team," Dmitri replied, feeling the correction was necessary, and immediately questioned himself on why that was so.

The vodka was eighty-proof ecstasy with a side order of heaven thrown in just to give it a little something special. It was at just the right temperature, which meant Svetlana had to have put the bottle into the freezer several hours before setting it on the table. Dmitri tried his level best to not stare at the mouthwatering amount of cleavage that Svetlana was showing, but she had a way of doing disastrous things to his willpower and self-control that made a very powerful man feel quite weak.

The urge to be a complete barbarian at that moment was almost overpowering to Dmitri. He wanted to let his inner Viking be set free. He wanted to pillage and plunder. He wanted to unleash his inner beast.

"You've always been handsome in my eyes," Svetlana said, "but never more so than right now. In uniform, you look . . . oh, I don't know what the right word is."

"Like a soldier?"

"No. Like a man. Like a *real* man."

The words added to the eroticism that Svetlana had created with the lingerie she had chosen to wear when greeting him at the door. In seconds, Dmitri was fully aroused, the front of his trousers swelling out, showing the length and girth he possessed when his desire was racing at redline but not yet out of control.

Svetlana looked down at the evidence of Dmitri's lust for her, and a sultry smile curled her mouth. With his free hand, Dmitri started to cover himself, but Svetlana shook her head and said quickly, "No. Don't hide."

She inhaled deeply, and when she exhaled slowly through her mouth, the mounds of her breasts trembled. She was staring now — unblinkingly — at Dmitri's erection, seemingly caressing it through his trousers with just her vision.

"I've seen it, you know," she said in a whisper. "And not just when I was stitching you up. In . . . in your sleep . . . after you had gotten better and were on the mend, you would get erections at night. I would look at it, but I never touched it."

Dmitri wanted to ask why she didn't — she was a long way from being a timid woman, he knew — but he didn't trust his own vocal cords to behave properly.

Svetlana turned and lifted her glass to place it onto the fireplace mantel, and when she did her décolletage separated the merest fraction of an inch more. The pale breast exposed to him at that instant was very nearly to her areola, and made his pulse pound like kettle drums in his temples . . . and in his erection.

"It seems," Svetlana said, turning once more to face Dmitri before her words stopped. "That is to say, you seem uncomfortable. Perhaps you'd let me help you become more at ease. At least for this evening. Would you like that?"

Again, not trusting his vocal cords, and certainly not what he no longer considered his better judgment, Dmitri nodded but remained otherwise silent.

Svetlana walked slowly around Dmitri until she stood directly behind him. "Careful with your glass now," she said as she reached up with both hands, easing them around Dmitri's biceps. Her fingers curled into the lapels of his jacket. "Spilling that vodka would be a crime against humanity." She began easing the jacket off Dmitri's shoulders. In a dichotomous way, her actions were simultaneously blatantly erotic and virginally innocent. "Or at least a crime against really good booze."

She slid the jacket down his left arm, waited until he had transferred the lowball glass to his right hand, then took the jacket off completely. With meticulous care, she folded the garment in half, so that the shoulders touched, and then placed it over the back of an overstuffed chair. The garment would not get wrinkled in its owner's absence. Every move that Svetlana made was meticulous.

She moved until she faced him again, then reached up and began loosening his necktie. Her fingers were deft, and Dmitri tried to not think too much about how she had acquired the skill. The thought of her being with another man would bring instant rage, and that was an emotion he didn't want at a time like this.

"Now that I've seen you in uniform, I know that every time from now on that I think of you, I'll see you in my mind's eyes wearing this uniform." She smiled with tender warmth, her eyes warm. "I'll also picture me taking it off you."

She pulled the necktie through the collars of his shirt, folded the necktie carefully in half, then placed it on his jacket.

When she returned to him her eyes glittered with an emotion Dmitri could only guess at. She began unbuttoning his shirt.

"You have such a broad chest. There's so much muscle. You must exercise all the time."

Dmitri didn't know if she expected him to answer her question, or consider it rhetorical. When he was with Svetlana, it seemed like everywhere he sailed was uncharted waters. Today was never anything like yesterday, and he had no idea at all what tomorrow would bring.

Her fingers had reached the last exposed button of his shirt, just above his belt buckle. She hesitated only a moment, then tugged his shirttails out of the waistband of his trousers and finished the unbuttoning. As with his jacket, she neatly folded it in half so that the shoulders aligned, then placed it on the chair. Dmitri watched every move with unblinking fascination. He was powerless to mentally focus on anything but her.

Dmitri took a sip of his drink and discovered that he had already drunk every drop of it. This stunned him. A cautious man, he always paid careful attention to how much and how quickly the alcohol went into his system.

"Let me refresh that for you," Svetlana said with faux casualness. When she took the glass from him, her fingers touched his and lingered for a second or two longer than necessary. The contact hadn't been long, but it had been intentional, and nothing less than electrifying for Dmitri.

Svetlana picked up her champagne flute from the mantel. It seemed to Dmitri that when she walked away from him to the table where the liquor was, there was a slight exaggeration in the sway of her hips as she moved. Though he stood motionless and outwardly at ease near the fireplace, his heart was hammering against his ribs, and the pulsing fury in his erection was the epitome of frustrated, wanton lust. He was a man at war with himself.

Svetlana slowly filled the drink glasses properly. Returning to Dmitri, she took a sip of her champagne before putting the glass on the mantel. She turned to Dmitri and rather deliberately stared at the swollen cock he had trapped inside the trousers of his uniform.

"I should have touched it while you were sleeping," she said, looking at Dmitri's cock instead of up into his eyes. Her voice was hardly more than a husky whisper. "At the very least that's what I should have done." Her breath caught in her throat. "But I'm afraid that sometimes, under certain circumstances, I'm not very good at taking the initiative in such matters."

She sank slowly to her knees, and for a second, Dmitri could neither inhale nor exhale. When, from on her knees, Svetlana looked up at him, the urge to grab her by the shoulders, throw her onto her back, and plunder her voluptuous curves with every bit of strength and virility he possessed right there on the floor was as strong as any emotion he had ever before experienced.

Svetlana untied the laces of Dmitri's dress shoes, removed them, then removed his socks. Sitting on the backs of her heels, she unbuckled his belt, unbuttoned his trousers, unzipped them slowly, then let them fall down around his ankles. Dmitri stepped out of them, and Svetlana folded them neatly and set them on the floor while remaining on her knees.

She placed her palms on Dmitri's hips, and looked up into his face. Very slowly, she leaned toward him, keeping eye contact the entire time. It wasn't until the last moment that she closed her eyes, turned her face directly toward him, and kissed the bulging erection that tented the fabric of his boxer-briefs.

It was the most erotic thing that Dmitri had ever seen.

CHAPTER SEVEN

As she kissed Dmitri's erection through his underwear, Svetlana wondered whether or not she had ever before truly wanted to suck a man's cock as much as she did at that very moment. When she was on assignment, giving blow jobs was sort of an obligation, something that simply had to be done if she was to successfully complete her mission. It was a chore that she was expected to fulfill, not really something that she looked forward to with breathless anticipation.

But Svetlana's mouth was watering with hungry anticipation. She could feel her clit tingling with rapidly escalating lust that was red-hot at the moment, but showed all the promise of becoming white-hot, and maybe even blindingly incandescent.

Svetlana eased her fingertips into Dmitri's elasticized waistband, then tugged the underwear down. When she got the boxer-briefs low enough, his cock sprang out. Though of course it did not make a sound, Svetlana could have sworn that she heard it sigh with relief upon being freed from its cotton prison.

She'd seen him erect before when he got nighttime erections. But never—not *ever*—had she seen him *this* hard. On her knees with his cock inches from her face, she could actually see a thick blue vein, which ran a swirling line along the shaft of the cock, pulsing visibly with Dmitri's rapid heartbeat.

Svetlana thought she should say something. After all, when one possessed a thing of such beauty, then surely that magnificence should be commented upon by those who saw it. And since her eyes were less than fifteen inches from the object of her admiration, she most definitely was seeing it. Every bit of it. In glorious detail. Up front, close and personal.

Without looking up, she whispered, "It's very big."

"I'll be careful."

Svetlana suspected that he'd said that more than a few times with women who were on their knees in front of him for the first time. In a bizarre way, since such emotions generally didn't go through her, she found herself harboring jealous emotions toward women she had never met, and never would.

What difference does it make to me if Dmitri has dispensed his considerable sensual charms with other women?

But like a lightning flash, marrow-deep resentment went through Svetlana. She was certain that, at that very moment, there were masturbating women who were closing their eyes and thinking back to the time when Dmitri had turned his connoisseur's sensual skills toward them, and they had reaped the benefits. They had trembled and shivered through the first orgasm, and had been thrilled by it . . . but not so much as they had enjoyed the second, third then four climaxes, all administered by a six-foot-four mountain of muscle and suave good charm.

Stop it. Stop it now. Svetlana's good judgment brought her rushing back to the real world, taking her away from insecurities and fears of things that would never come true.

Now that Dmitri was completely naked and his oh-so-impressive cock was pointed directly at her, Svetlana tilted her head back on her shoulders, looked him directly in the eyes, and said softly and with great sincerity, "I really wanted to do this to you when you were asleep, but you were recovering, and I didn't want to be a burden. But now that you're hale and hearty —" she raised her right hand and wrapped her fingers around the root of Dmitri's cock " — I see no reason why

I should deny myself."

In one swift move, Svetlana took as much of Dmitri's rigid, throbbing cock into her mouth as she could. She hadn't taken a slow and timid approach to giving a blow job. It was femininely forceful, rather more like a lioness than a kitten. She was a woman who knew exactly what she wanted, and she knew just how to get it.

She leaned toward Dmitri, shivering as she felt the delightful sensation of his hard cock, thick and throbbing with wanton desire, sliding between her lips, pressing against her tongue, rubbing against the roof of her mouth. She didn't stop until the swollen plum-sized head of Dmitri's cock was pressing demandingly against the opening of her throat, threatening to choke her by driving even deeper. On her knees, Svetlana squirmed.

Reaching between his powerful thighs, Svetlana brought her left hand palm-upward until she fondled the twin egg-shaped balls that would release their charge when she had given Dmitri enough pleasure. Cupping them in her hand, she squeezed them firmly as she applied, briefly, a particularly tight suction with her mouth on his cock.

"Oh," Dmitri sighed. "Oh, God . . . that's as good as I had dreamed it would be."

He's been dreaming of having me on my knees. The awareness made Svetlana's confidence soar and her passion rise to new heights. *This may be the first time for us, but it damn sure isn't going to be the last.*

"Kiss me."

It took several seconds before Svetlana was consciously aware that Dmitri had made a request—or was it a demand—of her. She was only too willing to accede to his authority.

With the pulsing head of his cock still in her mouth and throbbing against her tongue, she tilted her head back and looked up into his eyes, silently asking for a clarification of what had just been said. While on her knees for Dmitri, her intellectual acuity was rather less than lucid.

"I need you to kiss me," Dmitri said. "It's absurd that you're on your knees for me, but you've never been in my arms. I *need* to kiss you."

Svetlana had long believed that kissing mouth-to-mouth was infinitely more intimate for a woman to do with a man than it was to give him a blow job. Ten years in the service of Omega Force had more than confirmed this belief. So when Dmitri asked her to kiss him and her instant physical and emotional response was in the favorable to a factor of twenty or more, she knew deep down in her heart that her relationship with Dmitri wasn't merely professional, and it wasn't just raw, mindless lust. He wasn't just someone who could be of service to Omega Force, so therefore she would pretend to be enamored with him.

No. Not at all. Dmitri had crossed those barriers. He had climbed those walls. He was in elite company, and Svetlana knew this now.

And it scared the hell out of her.

Svetlana wasn't at all certain what role Dmitri would play in her life, but she was certain that his influence would be unforgettable. Unforgettable in the extreme.

"You," she said quietly, her breath against the moist crown of Dmitri's cock, "make me want to behave badly."

"You're exquisite when you're bad."

He always knows exactly what to say. He could talk me onto my knees in the middle of Izmaylovsky Park in Moscow at noon.

Conveniently, Svetlana pretended that she didn't have a strong exhibitionistic streak in her libido, and that giving Dmitri a blow job with a hundred people watching her wouldn't really be a wild turn-on for her. She was lying to herself and knew that she was, but accepted the fact that sometimes lies — even self-lies — were necessary.

I'll get on my knees to give him a blow job whenever he wants, wherever he wants.

Svetlana immediately realized that she must never think such things. They were dangerous in the extreme.

She tried to remind herself that Dmitri was a soldier in the Russian GRU, and that he was quite likely a mortal enemy that her own field supervisor, Jefferson Burke, could well assign her to assassinate . . . but this seemed difficult to emotionally grasp when she had the head of Dmitri's cock pressing against the opening of her throat, and she was telling herself that she would gladly swallow his cum, when that was an act of sexuality that she had done before, but seldom took any real pleasure in.

Suddenly, Dmitri bent at the waist and reached down, grabbing Svetlana by the upper arms. His grip seemed to have the power of steel. Svetlana winced, but she did not protest.

"I have more in mind for you than that," he said, his voice low and gravelly. "I want everything you have to give."

Svetlana tried to say that she was more than happy to have Dmitri take whatever he wanted to satisfy his wanton, barbarian needs, but she never got the chance. When Dmitri's large hand tightened around her biceps, at first she felt fear, because he was a very strong man, and his grip on her must surely be leaving bruises behind. But then he began lifting her. At first Svetlana rose to her feet. When she looked up into his face, she saw that his expression was one of granite determination. She thought that he looked exactly like a wolf that had visually locked onto his prey, and wouldn't stop until he, and his entire pack, had fed until all were satisfied.

He continued lifting her until her feet were no longer on the floor. With his elbows against his ribs, he raised her until her face was level to his. His eyes all but glowed with demonic desire.

"Kiss me," he said, his tone hoarse with sexual tension. "Kiss me like you mean it. I don't care if it's a lie. Kiss me like it's real."

Svetlana brought her mouth to his, and the first kiss that they shared was so feverish in its intensity that it was surprising lightning didn't shoot from their bodies. Svetlana opened her lips to receive Dmitri's tongue, and though this was the first time they had kissed so intimately, their tongues danced with a coordinated rhythm reserved for longtime lovers who had done this many times before.

For the first time since she was fourteen, Svetlana felt small. She actually felt petite as she dangled there in midair, her feet many inches from the floor, her arms at her sides as Dmitri held her tightly by the biceps. He held her without straining, as though she weighed nothing at all.

That first kiss eventually ended, but not before Svetlana's clit was pulsing with readiness, and the lips of her pussy were slick with her lusty juices. She was *so* ready for penetration.

With his lips brushing Svetlana's, Dmitri said, "Wrap your legs around me."

It was a demand that Svetlana readily complied with. When she locked her ankles together at the small of Dmitri's back, she was able to support her own weight.

"So powerful," Svetlana said as she looped her arms around his neck. His hands slipped down her back, caressing lightly until he cupped her bottom with both hands. Svetlana felt herself entering Valhalla. "I should be frightened of you, but I'm not." A moan escaped her. "I'm yours. Do with me whatever you wish."

She kissed him again, and it was much easier this time because with her arms and legs surrounding Dmitri, he didn't need to hold her so severely. Long seconds passed as Svetlana's tongue explored Dmitri's mouth, their lips forming a perfect seal, her hunger for him matched only by his hunger for her. Svetlana felt her nipples pressing against Dmitri's muscular chest, and his strong fingers as he squeezed and fondled the cheeks of her ass. Most evocatively. Svetlana felt the long, hard shaft of Dmitri's cock pressed against her, its heat seemingly going straight into her blood to warm it, heightening her arousal.

"Inside me," Svetlana said, taking her mouth away from Dmitri's to whisper into his ear. She felt a desperate, empty ache inside her. "I want you inside me." A shiver went through her. "I *need* you inside me."

Svetlana shivered when she realized how easy it was for Dmitri to accept her full weight as he moved his right hand to guide the head of his cock to her hungry sex. He lifted her a little higher to get at a more advantageous angle. A moment later the crown of his erection was starting to enter her as he lowered her body.

"Oh, God," Svetlana sighed, rolling her head back on her shoulders as she felt herself opening, yielding to Dmitri's great strength and lustful determination. "It feels heavenly to finally have you inside me." She opened her eyes briefly, found herself looking at the ceiling of her hotel room, then closed them again. "I dreamed of having your cock inside me . . . and now I do."

As Dmitri lowered her slowly, Svetlana could feel as inch by inch the thick shaft of his cock slipped between her labia, the solid flesh moving deeper and deeper into her hungrily receptive sex.

Svetlana relaxed the muscles in her thighs just enough to allow herself to slide down on Dmitri's impaling cock until she had taken all of him inside her slick passage. She felt a completeness, a connection to Dmitri, that was difficult for her to fathom.

"You're too good to be true," Svetlana whispered, her eyes closed as she felt Dmitri's cock throbbing with virility deep inside her. At that moment, she felt entirely filled with cock, stuffed to complete rapture. She could not want for anything more. "Bed . . . my bedroom is over there. This is heavenly, but I want to feel you on top of me."

She kept her eyes closed as Dmitri began walking. It occurred to her, in the strangely lucid way that happens when one part of the brain is completely disconnected from another part, and sexual bliss was not merely a wish but a real-world reality to be experienced in the here and now, that she was more than willing to let Dmitri do to her whatever he wanted. She would put no boundaries on his desire.

"Oh, God," she whispered into Dmitri's ear as he walked. Each step he took caused a new friction to tantalize Svetlana's hyper-aroused senses. She could feel, with shocking clarity, the throbbing, virile manliness that filled her pussy.

"Wait. Stop," Svetlana said suddenly, as spiraling emotions swirled through her overheating senses. "Don't take another step."

Dmitri stopped. Svetlana could sense him looking at her, no doubt wondering what had gone wrong. She kept her eyes closed, fearful of the expressing she might see on his face.

"Darling . . . my beautiful, barbarian darling," Svetlana whispered, vaguely understanding that what was happening now might never happen again in exactly the same way. "Fuck me standing up. I've done so many things . . . so many things that I'm not happy about and will never tell you. But I'm so close to climaxing, and no man has ever taken me the way you are now." A sob caught in her throat. "I'm begging you to make me come."

With her tongue, she drew Dmitri's earlobe between her teeth, then bit hard enough for him to gasp in pain.

"Fuck me," Svetlana said directly into his ear. "Later, in bed, you can make love to me. But right now, right here, I want you to fuck me . . . *hard*."

It was difficult for Svetlana to fully comprehend the fact that she had made such a bold statement. She wouldn't have believed she was capable of honestly saying such things if she had not heard those words spoken in her own voice. But she couldn't deny the truth of the words that had just passed between her lips.

Svetlana accepted the fact that she'd spoken boldly before, but almost always it was with someone she intended to seduce, then kill. With Dmitri it was different. She wasn't being intemperate in her dialog because the assignment Burke had sent her on required it. No, this time she was being emotionally honest, and that meant telling Dmitri exactly what she wanted him to do to her. And what she wanted, right then and there, was not loving and sensual and caring. It was raw, physical fucking.

He began raising and lowering her, lifting her until just the very tip of his cock's crown was still separating her pussy lips, then lowering her — almost dropping her — until he was fully embedded within her sheath and her legs were tight around his hips. His fingers dug deeply into the cheeks of her ass, gripping tightly.

"Oh, God, yesss," Svetlana whispered, feeling a climax rapidly approaching. "Just like that. Yes. Again and again and . . ."

Her words trailed off as her climax approached with shocking speed.

This thought had hardly gone through Svetlana's consciousness when she opened her mouth wide, and though she remained silent, the orgasm that ripped through her body was of such intensity that it was violent. She shook as the spasms went through her. Through her gyrations, Dmitri continued raising and lowering her, the muscles in his arms, legs, and torso all straining as his breath came in heated, labored gulps.

She had four powerful contractions, the second being more powerful than the first, then the third and fourth diminishing in intensity. But when the last contraction subsided, Svetlana could take no more stimulation without, she strongly suspected, suffering permanent physical damage. Surely, there must be a limit on how much stimulus a nerve ending could withstand.

"Stop," she gasped. "You've got to stop. I can't take any more of what you have to give." She sighed soulfully, clutching onto Dmitri. "That not true. I want more of you. Just . . . just give me some time."

To her supreme satisfaction, Dmitri did exactly as she had asked him to. She tightened her arms around his neck, her cheek against his temple, small tremors, like the aftershocks of an earthquake, going through her every couple seconds. There wasn't a nerve in her body that wasn't vibrantly, ecstatically alive.

They were motionless for nearly a minute, with Dmitri's body taut, his hands firm on Svetlana's bottom. She was coming down slowly from the sensual heights that Dmitri's extraordinary sexual prowess had taken her.

"I . . . I must be getting heavy for you," she said, as some small semblance of rationality returned to her.

"I could hold you like this, with me inside you, until the ends of time."

A shiver went through Svetlana. She desperately wanted to believe every word that Dmitri had just said, and the fact that she *wanted* to believe scared her to the marrow of her bones. She was on assignment from Omega Force, she reminded herself. When she was on assignment, she was supposed to be as coldly logical and without emotion as a computer. Emotions, particularly passionate ones, were to be avoided like the plague.

She kissed Dmitri's temple, and wasn't at all surprised when she discovered that he was perspiring. He had been holding her off the floor for some time, and she was not, by any measure, a tiny woman.

"Take me to *our* bed," she said softly, then ran the tip of her tongue around the circumference of Dmitri's ear. He shivered, and she was thrilled at the response she got. "Make love to me. I want to feel your weight upon me. Give me everything you have to give, and I'll give you everything I am."

It stunned her that she had spoken those words. It stunned her even more that she was speaking a truth that she could not comfortably acknowledge to herself on an intellectual level.

As he walked to the bedroom, with each step she felt his cock shifting and moving inside her. Never in her life had she felt so delicate, so petitely feminine. Dmitri's extraordinary strength touched her in a subtle, deeply sensual, womanly way that she had never before experienced.

Holding her bottom with one hand, he opened the door to her bedroom with the other. Svetlana kissed his cheek and temple, then both of his eyelids. There wasn't any part of him that she didn't want to kiss, didn't want to taste. She wanted to eat him alive, one little bite at a time.

Directly into his ear, as they stood at the side of her king-sized bed, she whispered, "Take me. I'm yours . . . to have however you want. There's nothing you can want that I won't give."

She had said such things before to men she needed to seduce because the mission demanded it, but this was the first time she had bared her soul so completely to a man she really did want to ravage her. With Dmitri, there were no boundaries—there were no limits to what, sexually, she wouldn't do for him.

Her emotions frightened her. They were unprecedented.

These things simply didn't happen to her.

Or so she thought . . . until Dmitri entered her life, then simply went about changing *everything*.

Carrying her effortlessly, Dmitri put a knee onto the

mattress, then moved Svetlana until she was in the middle of the bed.

When Dmitri lowered himself to press his chest against the mounds of Svetlana's breasts while his cock throbbed hotly, fully embedded inside her, Svetlana purred, "Yesss. Oh, yesss."

Dmitri started to move, but Svetlana stopped him.

"Not yet," she whispered her arms tight around his neck. "Soon . . . but not yet. Let me savor the feel of you filling me. Just for a little while . . . then you can fuck me like the barbarian you are."

She bit his earlobe hard enough to cause pain.

I'm going to pay a price for that.

She almost giggled at the prospect.

Directly into Dmitri's ear, Svetlana whispered, "Let's make love another time. This time I want you to fuck me. Hard."

Svetlana got exactly what she asked for.

Dmitri was as forceful, as dominating, as she had hoped he would be. In the middle of the king-size bed, with her legs wrapped around his waist, Dmitri churned his hips like an out of control steam engine. She bounced on the bed, the breath being forced from her lungs each time Dmitri rammed full-length into her, her body literally bouncing under the onslaught of the harsh, erotic, utterly masculine lovemaking.

"Yes," Svetlana heard herself say between jolting downward thrusts of Dmitri's hips. "This is . . . what I want . . . from you." It was difficult to speak being pummeled as she was.

Dmitri slanted his mouth down over hers. It was a bruising, demanding kiss that took possession of her body, heart, and soul. Svetlana tightened her arms around his neck, hugging him tightly, loving the feel of his hot, labored breath against her cheek as he writhed in ecstasy above her.

"Come for me," she said, the words coming out taut with the sexual tension she felt. "Come inside me."

But it wasn't Dmitri who climaxed next, it was Svetlana. Her eyes suddenly opened wide, then her mouth did, though she remained silent. Her body began convulsing, her pussy flexing and contracting around the solid column of masculinity that filled it time and time again.

And then Svetlana heard a high-pitched wail of ecstasy. It was the sound of a woman screaming, and it took a moment before she realized she was the woman who was screaming. The climax that Dmitri had driven her to was more powerful than she had thought any could be.

She was just coming down from the heights of her passion when Dmitri thrust full length into her, then uttered a low, rumbling groan of passion and became still between her parted thighs. Svetlana smiled at the thought that his semen was now inside her, and that she had satisfied him.

"Yes," she whispered, stroking the back of Dmitri's head as his body, seemingly now very heavy, became limp upon hers

"Don't move. Just savor the moment." She kissed his cheek. His weight felt wonderful. His chest dominated her. "That was beautiful. You are beautiful."

Is this what heaven feels like?

The question slithered through Svetlana's consciousness. She was in bed, and drifting somewhere between being awake and being asleep. Part of her wanted to go back into a deep sleep, but part of her *really* wanted to be fully awake so that she could experience every subtle nuance of what was being done to her.

Her clit had always been sensitive. Svetlana suspected that it was more sensitive than the ones other women had. She had no empirical evidence to back up this belief. In fact, she had no way of testing this theory in any kind of scientifically valid manner. She just suspected that her clit was more finely tuned to receiving pleasure than those of her peers.

This thought was going through her mind as she floated blissfully in the ether of sexual satisfaction.

"Ohhh."

It took several seconds for Svetlana to become aware of the fact that she herself had made the sound.

And why had she done that? Hmmm?

Warm, soft lips surrounded her clit, then sucked lightly upon it, while a tongue moved slowly side to side against it. The sensation wasn't fiercely erotic, but rather gently sensual. The person sucking and licking lightly upon her clit was in no hurry to have her climax, and for that she was endlessly grateful.

Svetlana opened her eyes, and through the fan of her lashes looked down between the mounds of her breasts to see, between her upraised thighs, Dmitri. All she could see of him, though, was from the nose upward. His mouth was hidden from her because it was pressed against her pussy.

No man has ever been so handsome. It's not fair that he's that good looking.

In stark emotional contrast to her previous thought, she said, "Suck."

Svetlana heard the single word spoken aloud. Had she been fully awake, she would have been embarrassed with her selfishness. A lady didn't say things like *suck* when it had to do with her clitoris. So when she heard herself say, with a bit more determination and forcefulness, *Eat me* she was quite surprised. And a little embarrassed. Actually, rather more than a little embarrassed, though the emotion didn't last long.

As though from a great distance, though she knew this was most certainly not the case, she heard a familiar, masculine voice say, in a slightly muffled manner under the circumstance, "Close your eyes and go back to sleep."

It seemed to be a perfectly logical, reasonable request. She closed her eyes, but she continued to float through the clouds of half-sleep as her clit was gently orally stimulated.

Can I come without actually waking up . . . will I?

Eleven minutes later, Svetlana discovered that she could, in fact, have a thoroughly satisfying climax without ever completely gaining consciousness. Approximately thirty seconds after her orgasm, with the most serene of smiles on her lips, she passed into the deepest, most satisfying sleep of her life.

Virile men had erections when they slept. It was just something that happened to healthy men. Sometimes men were aware of it when they got an erection, and sometimes they weren't. Most times they weren't. Generally, the hard-ons came and went without notice. That was just the way the human anatomy worked.

But this time Dmitri's nighttime erection was different. He wasn't awake, really, but he wasn't really asleep, either. Still, he was quite certain that this erection was different from all the others that had come to him while he slept.

It took several seconds for him to understand exactly *what* was different about this erection. Had he been fully awake, he would have known instantly, but since he wasn't, it took several seconds for him to clarify the difference.

Lips.

Soft, feminine lips.

And a moist, wet suction that went along with those lips.

Fuck. Seriously?

Dmitri opened his eyes and found himself staring at the ceiling of a luxury hotel room that he couldn't afford in this or any other lifetime. Very slowly, he let his gaze roam downward. Eventually, gloriously, he found himself looking into the sea blue eyes of Svetlana. She smiled with her eyes, but not with her mouth. Her eyes—the most beautiful in all the planets of the universe, Dmitri was willing to swear at that moment—were bright, and in them was erotic amusement. She did not smile with her lips, because at that moment they were surrounding the shaft of Dmitri's cock. He could feel her tongue moving from side to side against the underside of the head of his cock.

"To say good morning would be a colossal understatement," Dmitri said, his voice gravelly with sleep.

With a slurping sound, Svetlana allowed Dmitri's cock to slip out of her mouth. Her actions, Dmitri could tell, were meant to be seen as well as felt. She kissed the head of his cock, licked it several times like an ice cream cone, then smiled at him.

"Go back to sleep. I know you're tired, but you had this lovely erection and it seemed to me that it needed some attention." Her eyes took on a sudden seriousness. "Something as beautiful as this shouldn't be ignored, should it?"

Dmitri tried to speak, found he couldn't, and then simply shook his head.

"Go back to sleep," Svetlana said as she resumed licking Dmitri's cock, from the base up to the head, then back down again. "You're still recovering from being shot. You need all the sleep you can get."

Dmitri closed his eyes, but he did not go back to sleep.

"We'd like four eggs, scrambled, with four pieces of toast, buttered on one side. We need four strips of bacon, and four sausage links. And we need an order of diced fried potatoes, done extra crispy. We also need a carafe of coffee, and a glass of orange juice, one of tomato juice, and one of milk."

While holding the room service phone to her ear, Svetlana looked at Dmitri and asked, "Can you think of anything else that you might want?"

"Aren't you having anything for breakfast?"

Svetlana shook her head. "I had a high protein energy drink earlier."

CHAPTER EIGHT

With his telephone pressed tightly to his ear, Dmitri said, "You're sure? You're absolutely sure?"

"He's in the Seine Hotel in Paris. Don't know just yet how long he's been there," General Lebedev said. "Finish the job, Dmitri. There are a lot of powerful people paying attention to this, and nobody wants to see another day go by when Boris is still alive."

"Understood, sir," Dmitri said, the phone to his ear, his left hand over his heart.

Dmitri turned to Svetlana, who was in bed with the blanket around her waist. Her breasts — her beautiful, magnificent breasts that Dmitri simply couldn't get enough of — were exposed to his greedy gaze. But, for once, he hardly paid them any attention at all.

"We found him," he said. "He's in Paris."

Paris, France

Boris set down his coffee cup on the ledge of his hotel balcony and thought for a moment how good it felt to be back in Paris. He'd always felt contentment here. He looked down at the Avenue des Champs-Elysees, and a faint smile curled his lips. When was the first time he'd seen the Arc de Triomphe? Sixteen? Maybe younger than that? And now he had a hotel room that overlooked the Arc. A hotel room that cost him more a night than he used to make in months.

I've been lucky, but the only reason I've been lucky is because I've been smart. I looked at every deal I came across from both sides. I knew what they wanted and I didn't let anyone stand in my way. From the very beginning, I always came out on top. I always turned a profit.

His room telephone rang. Boris looked at it. He'd used his cell phone since his escape from Ukraine. After what happened in Kiev, his first instinct had to go underground, and that had been a smart move.

Gunfire and bloodshed were always bad business, no matter how one looked at it. Necessary or not, blood was always an ugly matter. Boris was glad to be away from Kiev. Occurrences like that were always best left in the past.

Boris touched the button to connect the inbound call.

"Yes?"

"There's someone here that I think you might like to see." The voice was familiar to Boris. It was the night manager of a hotel he frequented when in town.

"Why?"

"Because she's tall with hair as black as midnight, milk white skin, she's beautiful, has a dozen credit cards that have no limit, and she's drinking like she trying hard to forget something or someone. I just thought that you'd like to be the man to lift her spirits."

"There's going to be an extra little something in your next envelope. Please send me the security video to my phone, and whatever other information you have."

"Of course, sir. I'm sending it now."

Boris looked out the car window at the tall buildings that surrounded both sides of the street. Since Kiev, he was especially careful regarding his own personal safety. He still didn't know exactly what had happened in that outdoor saloon, other than he had assigned three men to interrogate—and then kill—a man who may or may not have been following him. What was certain was that all three of his bodyguards had gotten themselves very dead in one hell of a hurry, and whoever had killed them had yet to be apprehended. Some reports said it was a man who kill them. Others said it was a woman. Boris suspected that somewhere there was an eyewitness who would swear it was a Martian.

Boris waited until Pavel opened the rear door to the sedan for him, then he stepped out onto the sidewalk in front of the hotel. He looked left and right at the people walking. Some were tourists. They had that carefree, unhurried look to them. Most of the foot traffic were locals, either shopping or coming home from work. They were more mentally focused on what they were doing.

The hotel's night manager was behind the front desk, and when he spotted Boris, he immediately signaled for his second-in-command to take over the desk. He hurried to meet Boris face to face.

"I think you'll like her," the bald-headed, pot-bellied man in the immaculate grey suit said, keeping his voice low. Such matters weren't to be discussed too loudly, and certainly not in front of strangers. "She got here yesterday morning, but I didn't know about her arrival until earlier this evening. When I saw her, I knew that you needed to be notified immediately."

"Smart move," Boris said. The hotel bar was off to the left of the main lobby. The entrance was very wide, and the interior very dark. Boris had been there several times, but so far he hadn't found female companions to entertain him for more than a night. As he got older, he was being more selective. "You say she seems to have her own money? She's not in it for money?"

"No, sir. I did a background check just like I always do whenever someone is booking in our more exclusive rooms.

She has sterling credit, though her background is questionable in places."

Boris's brow furrowed. "Questionable? I don't know what that means."

"There are gaps in her personal history that are unaccounted for. What I can say with certainty is that she has no criminal background. If she did, then I would have discovered it."

"And she's not underage?" Boris had to be careful about that. He'd known more than just a few powerful men who had their entire lives and careers destroyed because they couldn't be satisfied with women of a legal age. It was a mistake he never intended to make.

"She's south of thirty," the night manager said. He smiled. "But not by much."

What the hell is she doing alone in a bar, drinking more than she should?

It was a tantalizing question for Boris to consider.

"What did you say her name was?"

"Svetlana Simonov. She took a room without advance notice, and she's booked through the end of the week, though she says her stay could go longer than that."

"You're going to get a nice envelope this week," Boris said, then turned away from the night manager. Boris often hired men like the night manager, but he didn't like spending any more time with them than was absolutely necessary. In his world, they were what he thought of as a necessary evil.

With his new bodyguards in front of and behind him, Boris stepped into the saloon. Electronic dance music was playing, though not overly loud. Several couples were dancing in the herky-jerky fashion that fit the music. Boris dismissed the couples as insignificant. The men were in their thirties, and the women were in their twenties. None of them had the look of power and wealth that Boris required. Men with real power didn't dance to EDM.

It didn't take long for Boris to spot the woman he had been told about. She was as beautiful as the night manager had said she was, with midnight black hair that cascaded over her shoulders and fell down the front of her body to obscure the fullness of her bosom. Even from a distance and in the dim light of the tavern, Boris could see that she was strikingly beautiful, with large blue eyes and a generous mouth that hinted at indiscretions. She had broad shoulders. Significantly sized diamond earrings showed in both earlobes, and if the woman hadn't been so beautiful, or if she had been much younger, Boris would have suspected the diamonds were really just glass.

Those are real diamonds. More than two carats. Probably closer to three. And her tits are real, too. There isn't anything about her that isn't real.

The woman was sitting motionless in the booth, her hands flat on the tabletop, looking at her martini glass that still had most of a drink and three stuffed olives in it. Boris watched as a man in his middle-forties, sporting a comb-over to try to hide the fact that he was losing his hair, approached the booth and said something to the woman. For several seconds she continued staring at her drink, but then her gaze roamed upward to the man's face. She shook her head. It was the faintest of gestures, but with it she had dismissed the man so thoroughly and completely it was as though he had never existed.

Leaning back against the bar, Boris studied the woman. Something was bothering her, and Boris suspected that if he had any chance at all in getting her into his hotel room, he had to figure out what it was *before* he introduced himself to her.

"Bartender, what excellent champagne do you have on hand and chilled?"

"Bollinger's, Tattainger's, and Dom Perignon. Good years for all three," the bartender answered with the confidence of a man in the service industry who knew exactly what he was doing. "To order them you've got to buy full bottles. No half-bottles."

Boris gave the man an icy look to indicate that he *never* ordered half-bottles of champagne, and that he didn't like the assumption that he did.

"Sorry, sir," the bartender, quite chastened, said immediately. "Bit of a habit to say. Again, I'm sorry. Meant no disrespect."

"Don't worry about it," Boris said, then smiled, his superior status established to his satisfaction. "Use your best judgment on the champagne. I'd like two glasses and the bottle on ice brought to that woman there." Boris nodded toward the raven-haired woman who sat alone with her thoughts in a booth that could seat six. "Is there caviar with toast available?"

"Yes, sir."

"Good. But don't bring it to the table until I order it."

"Of course, sir. Naturally."

Boris waited until the champagne in the ice bucket arrived and when the waiter delivered it, the woman smiled a little and looked around the saloon to find out who her benefactor was. When she made eye contact with Boris, he dipped his head a fraction of an inch in acknowledgement. She raised her glass, and that was all the invitation that Boris needed. He crossed the room slowly as she watched him. He knew he was at the top of his game.

If a five hundred euro bottle of champagne isn't an impressive calling card, then nothing is.

Boris knew both when and how to play a trump card.

At the table, Boris said, in English, "Forgive me for being so bold, but you seemed a bit melancholy, and in my experience, Bollinger's chases away melancholy better than almost anything else on the planet."

"You are a wise man," the woman said in English, but with a distinct Russian accent. "Would you like to sit down?" Together we will find out if this year's vintage is worth the reputation it has."

Introductions were made. They had drunk half the bottle when Svetlana began explaining that she was in Paris because she was running away from a hopelessly complicated romance situation in Washington D.C., where she had fallen quite completely in love with a Mr. and Mrs. Carpenter, who together owned a chain of very profitable clothing stores, and together explained to Svetlana that they had found a young woman who could not only serve as their babysitter, but could also sexually satisfy both of them. And did. Nightly. Her youth and energy were really quite astonishing. Both of them said so with heartfelt sincerity.

"They didn't have to be so specific," Svetlana said as Boris topped off her champagne glass for the third time. "Telling me just how young and beautiful she is was nothing less than an act of cruelty, don't you think?"

"A woman like you should never have been treated like that," Boris said, finding it utterly thrilling that Svetlana had been knee-deep in a three-way love affair with both a man and a woman. The fact that they were married only added spice for Boris's palate. "If you were my lady, I'd treat you with the respect you deserve."

He knew that she'd been drinking, though he didn't know how much she'd had prior to his arriving at her booth. Boris liked it when his women drank alcohol. It so often helped them to shed inhibitions they otherwise clutched like a life jacket when the waves got choppy.

"It seems to me that I've met you somewhere before," Boris said. The thought had been toying with his consciousness for some time. "I just can't seem to put my finger on where I've seen you before."

"It's never a good thing to tell a woman you can't remember where you first met her," Svetlana said, the corners of her mouth turning downward in disapproval. "A woman always wants to be remembered."

"Of course," Boris said, hoping like hell that he hadn't just made an unforgivable error. He knew better than to tell a woman she was forgettable. "I'm sure that if we'd met, I would recall everything about the memorable day."

Svetlana smiled at him, drank the last swallow of her champagne, then held her glass out. Boris was more than happy to refill her glass. As he did so, holding the bottle in his right hand, he placed his left palm lightly on Svetlana's leg, midway between her knee and hip. He watched as she inhaled sharply upon his touch, but she made no move to push his hand away. Boris took that as a good sign. A *very* good sign. His hand was only inches away from her pussy, and they both knew it.

The flesh beneath his palm was the texture of velvet. Warm velvet. When he looked into Svetlana's eyes, he thought them to be the deepest blue that he had ever seen, and he wondered who in hell would possibly turn this woman away . . . for a *babysitter?*

He still had his hand on Svetlana's naked thigh when she picked up her small purse and, from inside, extracted a tube of lipstick. Though he had watched women before apply lipstick, he could not think of a time when it had seemed quite so erotic as it did at that moment.

When Svetlana returned the lipstick to her purse, she turned slightly toward Boris. There was a brightness in her eyes that Boris found more than just a little enticing, even inviting. The atmosphere in the booth had changed. What had been romantic potential was now erotic probability.

"Whenever I know I'm going to be kissed, I always refresh my lipstick," Svetlana said, her voice just barely audible above the piped-in electronic dance music. "A woman should always be wearing the absolutely right shade of lipstick, don't you think? I think men appreciate that."

Boris leaned toward Svetlana, half expecting her to

suddenly pull away, but she did not. She really *was* as bold as she had led him to believe. He kissed her mouth lightly at first. He didn't want to push his luck by going for more than what she might be offering.

And, most erotically, she had not spoken so much as a single word about money, or asked what he did for a living or how he made his money. Boris had become hardened to the women who pretended to be turned on by him as a man when he really knew that all they were interested in was getting a slice of the financial pie that he was. Financially, he was a big fucking pie. With whipped cream on top. And a lot of women wanted a piece of that pie.

He touched her lips with the tip of his tongue. It was a delicate move, intended to question without making any demands. When just a second or two later he felt her tongue touch his, Boris felt his cock come immediately to life, stretching and growing more swiftly than it had in years. She had stripped a dozen years from his libido in a single kiss. Svetlana wasn't like those girls who had come and gone through his life over the past years, she was a full-grown woman who apparently knew what she wanted and wasn't afraid to go for it. And there wasn't anything about her that didn't turn him on to the very marrow of his bones.

Boris ended the kiss, but not until a full thirty seconds had passed. He looked up and to his left. Pavel and the other two gunmen were standing nearby, mostly watching the crowd, but also keeping an eye on him.

"Stand in front of me," Boris said to Pavel. "Side by side."

Without saying a word, the three newly hired men moved so that they were shoulder-to-shoulder, blocking the view of the other patrons from the activities happening in Boris's booth. The men were new to Boris's employment, but they knew what their job was, and they knew how to do it.

"Kiss me again," Svetlana said, placing her palm lightly on

Boris's cheek. "You know how a woman wants to be kissed. Most men don't."

Boris kissed her, and this time he slanted his mouth down more firmly over Svetlana's, his tongue exploring her mouth more deeply. As he kissed her, his tongue toying with hers, he slid his palm a little higher up her naked thigh, now pushing the bottom hem of her minidress upward to make room for his bold caress.

Svetlana turned her face aside to end the kiss. She was breathing deeply, and Boris could tell that her passion was running hot. Perhaps not as feverishly as his, but there was nothing about how she was responding to his seduction that said anything other than that her passion was racing.

Boris kissed her throat, then bared his teeth and nipped her with his incisors. Svetlana uttered a soft squeal of protest, but made no move to push his away.

Boris slid his hand higher on her thigh, not stopping until his fingers were pressed against her panties. He could feel the heat of her cunt through the thin barrier of cotton, and his lust surged even higher.

"Stop," Svetlana gasped, the single word whispered, but carrying with it the frantic quality of a woman suddenly and desperately out of her emotional comfort zone. "Please, don't make me beg. You've got to stop."

Boris rubbed his fingers against the lips of her pussy through her panties, his lust soaring to new heights. He didn't care if he had to fuck her right there on the dance floor with the whole world watching. He *had* to have her.

"Stop," Svetlana said again, but this time when she said it, she reached down and wrapped her fingers around Boris's wrist. She pulled his hand out from between her spread thighs. "I said stop."

"What? Why?"

Boris was quite willing to throw her to the hard floor and

fuck her, whether she wanted him to or not. Women simply didn't get him all hot and bothered, then say the whole thing had been a mistake. That was the kind of behavior that he had never tolerated in women, and he wasn't averse to using his fists to get his point across.

"I've had too much to drink," Svetlana said, looking into his eyes. "Tomorrow, I want you to come to my room. Come see me, and bring your men." She took his hand and brought it to her mouth. Slowly, lewdly, she licked his palm, then licked along his middle finger until she reached the tip. Lastly, while looking him in the eyes, she sucked on his finger in a pantomime of fellatio.

"What room are you in?"

Svetlana told him.

"Tomorrow, when I haven't had so much to drink, I'll make you a happy man. But I can't tonight. I'm sorry." She licked his palm again. She did it in a manner that was nothing less than obscene. "Tomorrow at noon I'll give you everything you've ever wanted in a woman. And if you want your men to watch, they can. I'll even do them, too, if you want to watch. But it's got to be tomorrow."

To Boris's profound fury, Svetlana slipped out of the booth. Hurrying across the dance floor, she disappeared into the crowd.

CHAPTER NINE

She'd better be ready to fuck the instant I walk through the door.
The previous evening, after Svetlana had run away, Boris
had stared at the ceiling, his cock hard as stone but without a
warm, feminine body to shove into. The fact that he had allowed Svetlana to get him wildly around, then not satisfy the
desire that she had provoked, was a reality that Boris could
hardly comprehend. Even when he had been poor he hadn't
allowed women to treat him that way. And he sure as fuck
wasn't going to allow it now.

For a couple seconds, as he stood in front of Svetlana's hotel room door, Boris breathed slowly in and out, forcing himself to relax. Svetlana had an infuriating way of making him
feel very young and quite insecure, like he had when he was
a teenager, and the most popular, attractive girls didn't want
to have anything to do with him.

If she thinks she can be a cock-teaser and not pay the price, she's
dead fucking wrong. I'll blacken both of her eyes if that's what's nec-
essary to teach her who the fucking boss is.

He rapped his knuckles against the door, and when it
opened immediately, Boris knew that she had been waiting at
the door for his arrival. That was a good sign. Maybe he
wouldn't need to use his fists on her after all.

The next good sign was how she was dressed to receive
him. She had already done her hair and makeup, he noted immediately, but she hadn't actually gotten dressed. She wore a
white silk robe that covered her down to mid-thigh. The silk
was thinner than paper and proved without doubt that she

was not wearing a brassiere. The shape of her nipples was on display, and the breath caught in Boris's throat for just a moment because of it.

"Good morning," he said.

"I'm not much of a morning person," Svetlana replied, giving him a smile, then gazing quickly and dismissively at the bodyguards who accompanied him. Her eyes said without words that she was only interested in the man in power. "I prefer waking up at noon." She smiled warmly. "But for you, I got up at eleven. I wanted to do my hair and makeup, though I couldn't quite figure out what you'd like me to wear." She squared her shoulders and ran her hands down her sides. "I hope this will please you, at least until I can figure out what clothes you'd like to see me in." She looked away for a moment. "Unless I decide to get some sun. Then you'll have to have your men be somewhere other than on the balcony. This hotel has the loveliest balcony, and at noon the sun is absolutely perfect."

She stepped aside to let Boris and his men enter her luxury suite of rooms. The urge to fondle her breasts, hidden only by the sheerest silk on the planet, was overloading Boris's senses with a tsunami of erotic impulses.

I'm going to fuck her on the floor. Then I'm going to fuck her in bed. Then I'm going to make her suck my cock while Pavel and his crew watches.

Now that his thoughts and intentions were clear in his own mind, Boris felt more at ease. Svetlana might have toyed with him on the previous evening, but she wasn't going to on this day. From this moment forward, Boris was going to be in charge of his world and everyone in it, and if Svetlana didn't like it, then she was in for a long and very nasty and brutal day of debauchery the likes of which she would never, ever forget.

"I like to have mimosas for breakfast," Svetlana said as she closed the door behind the bodyguards, "but if you'd like something more substantial, I can pour that, too."

Boris was surprised that Svetlana was going to start her day at noon, and with alcohol — but only a little surprised. He had seen the way she gulped her cocktails the previous night, and even then he didn't know how much she had drunk prior to his arrival at the saloon.

She's not the first lush I've fucked, and she won't be the last.

He decided that Svetlana would stay in his life — and, most significantly, in his bed — for two to three weeks. By that time she'd start making demands and having expectations of him, and that was something he never tolerated in his bedmates. Not even ones as beautiful as Svetlana.

Boris watched as Svetlana walked to a wheeled liquor tray and poured champagne into a glass, then filled it with ice. Lastly, she filled the glass to the rim with orange juice.

As she returned to him, Boris watched her breasts moving erotically beneath her silk robe, and he felt his lust surging to life. He decided that Svetlana might be alcoholic, but her lusty charms were beyond question.

He wanted to fuck her more than he had wanted to fuck any woman in years.

She handed him his cocktail, then said, "I'm assuming that your men know how to pour themselves whatever they want. Now I'd like to get some sun, so you can please tell your men they're supposed to stay in the living room while we're out on the balcony." She took a sip of her mimosa, sighed with satisfaction, and gave Boris a smile that hinted at mischief. "I don't mind giving them a bit of a show, but I'd rather not be ogled." With her left hand, she untied the sash surrounding her waist. The silk opened slightly, showing the inner slopes of her breasts. "I don't like tan lines, so I always get naked in the sun."

With a shrug of her shoulders, her robe filtered down her arms and fell to the floor. And though Boris was a man of considerable experience with very attractive women, when he got to see Svetlana wearing only a pair of white bikini panties, his heart began pounding, and his lust kicked into high gear.

"You don't mind if I let your men see what you're soon to have, do you?" Her smile was deceptively innocent. "I thought I'd keep the panties on until you and I are alone on the balcony. Then, if you want, you can take them off." She turned and started walking toward the balcony. "Actually, you can do whatever you want with me," she said, her voice loud enough for all four men to hear. "I don't mind your men seeing my pussy, but only you get to fuck it."

This is the woman I've waited for my entire life, the one I've always wanted but never found. Until now. Damn, I can't make up my mind about her.

Svetlana turned toward Boris's men, her naked breasts and feminine body on bold display.

"I'm counting on you to stay in here. No peeking, because there's the very real possibility that I'm going to be giving him a blow job after I have a couple of drinks. And if I have *more* than a couple of drinks, I might be giving blow jobs to all of you." Boris watched as her eyes narrowed, as though she was trying very hard to make herself seem formidable. "But only if Boris tells me to, and only if you don't do any peeking while I'm getting some sun." She turned to Boris, smiled softly, and said, "I only suck cock after I've had a couple drinks. You don't mind, do you?" She shrugged, and her breasts wobbled. "You won't have to wait long. I'll drink fast."

Boris was looking at Svetlana's ass, lovingly embraced with white bikini panties, as she walked through the room, then out the glass doors and onto the balcony. At that moment, he was quite certain that he'd never met a woman as exciting as Svetlana, and that he never would again. She was in a league by herself.

He looked at his men. The expression on their faces told the story of their shock at what they had just witnessed, and their profound envy of Boris's good fortune. It was *exactly* the way that Boris wanted it.

"I'll let you know when I'm done with her," he said, keeping his voice low enough so that Svetlana couldn't hear. "You can all fuck her however you want to, but not until I've had my fill."

Pavel cleared his throat, then replied, "Yes. Of course, sir. You write the rules. We all know that."

Svetlana stretched out on the padded recliner on the balcony, closed her eyes, and tried hard to not be scared out of her mind.

Surreptitiously, she lowered her right hand, which held her glass of champagne and orange juice, and poured the contents out. Then, lifting the glass to her mouth, she pretended to drink the last of its contents.

"Darling, would you make me another?" She raised the empty glass as though she had done something noteworthy by drinking it. "Then come out and sit beside me. What's the point in me taking of my clothes if you're not here to look at me?"

She laughed in a vaguely alcoholic way, and her champagne flute was quickly snatched from her hand.

In little more than a minute, Boris was back to her with a freshly made mimosa, and a bulge in his trousers that said he very much enjoyed the erotic game that Svetlana was playing for his pleasure.

When Boris returned with her glass, Svetlana stretched and yawned in feline fashion to put her naked breasts on prominent display, took her drink from him, and said in a sensual purr, "Now sit down beside me and together we'll enjoy the sunshine. By the way, I didn't really mean it when I said I'd fuck your men. That was just something I threw out so that they would be jealous of the good times that I'm going to show you."

Svetlana looked at the hotel across the street. It was two stories taller than the hotel she was staying at. The distance separating them was little more than a hundred yards.

She felt Boris put his hand on her left breast, capturing her nipple between his forefinger and thumb. He pinched a little harder than he should have, but Svetlana forced herself to neither wince no show any dissatisfaction with his behavior.

"Be patient, darling," she said. "I told you, I'm only an enthusiastic cocksucker if I've had a couple drinks first. Trust me, you're not going to have to wait long to get exactly what you deserve."

She opened her eyes and turned her head to look at Boris. He had just settled back on the recliner next to hers when she heard the bullet hit him in the chest. His arms and legs straightened in a spasm, but then he went entirely limp and was motionless. Svetlana did not hear the sound of the rifle's report, because Dmitri had told her he was going to use a silencer. The bullet had been hollowed out by an armorer at GRU, and then filled with liquid mercury before being re-tipped with lead. Upon impact, as the bullet slowed, the mercury rushed forward, causing the bullet to fragment, quadrupling the lethality of the round.

A half second after a fragmenting bullet ripped apart all the vital orgasms in his chest cavity, the second bullet hit home, striking Boris in the forehead. Literally everything from his nose upward virtually disintegrated. When Boris's head exploded, it sent fragments of bone, brains, and blood splashing outward in a three foot circle.

Svetlana was covered in what had been in Boris's head.

She felt the urge to vomit, but suppressed the urge.

She knew she'd never forget the sound of the bullet hitting Boris's forehead.

If my cover's intact, I'll live. If it's not, Dmitri's next bullet is for me.

She waited, hardly breathing, for the bullet that she would never hear. She prayed that on the rooftop across the street, Dmitri was disassembling his rifle and putting it away in the specially designed suitcase.

The urge to wipe away the blood, brains, and fragmented bone from her face and torso was almost overpowering, but Svetlana knew what had to be done. She began counting to one thousand. It was necessary to give Dmitri enough time to disassemble his assassin's rifle and to get out of the hotel across the street. Only then, when he had made his escape, could she begin the next phase of the successful assassination.

This was not the time to get impatient.

When she counted to seven hundred, Svetlana got out of the recliner, and turned toward the glass doors. She saw her reflection and promised herself she'd dye her hair back to streaked blonde as soon as she could. Then she walked to the doorway leading into her hotel room and began to scream. Boris's bodyguards hurried out onto the balcony to see the nearly headless corpse of the man who had been paying their wages.

"I'm fucking out of here. That bastard can't pay anybody," Pavel said as he hurried to the hotel room door, with his subordinates close at his heels.

Svetlana counted to thirty, then she took off her panties and walked out onto the balcony, careful to not raise her gaze enough to see what remained of the man she despised. She put her panties in his right hand, then walked out of her room.

She began shouting in the hallway and didn't stop screaming until she was in the hotel's lobby, and there were more than a dozen people around her.

The gory remains of what had been inside Boris's head was dripping down her naked body.

The day manager of the hotel did a quick background check of Boris, and on Svetlana, and the only thing he was absolutely certain of was that he wanted nothing to do with either of them. Svetlana was told to shower, and her suitcases were packed for her. Then she was driven to the airport, accompanied by the day manager and a member of the hotel's security team. Her passport had been used recently, and though she was far from sober, which was supposed to be a requirement for boarding a plane, the hotel bought her a one-way ticket on the first flight out of Paris. Literally within minutes of arriving at the airport, Svetlana was comfortably seated in first class, headed for Havana, Cuba.

Despite the way she had pretended to slur her words in the hotel, she was now quite sober.

I wonder if Dmitri's thinking of me.

She suspected she would not forget him anytime soon. Or at all. Ever. All she was truly certain of was that she would never say a word about Dmitri to Burke.

The End

YOU MAY ALSO ENJOY THE FOLLOWING FROM EXTASY BOOKS INC:

Double Trouble
Robin Gideon

Excerpt

"I'm sorry," Burke said, his lips temporarily compressed. "Something has come up that's requiring immediate attention. We've got to act on it instantly because every second counts." He looked at Svetlana, then at Tatiana. "This is a bad one. One of the worst security breeches I've ever seen."

Svetlana felt a chill go through her. Burke wasn't the kind of man who exaggerated the danger of a situation. Not when it came to national security.

A waitress stepped forward, though she remained about ten feet from the booth. Svetlana realized that Burke had given her forewarning that privacy was to be maintained.

"We'd like a round," Burke said.

Svetlana watched him smile, and immediately saw the waitress's favorable response to it. For several seconds she had to try very hard to not resent the young woman for responding romantically to Burke's gorgeous smile.

"For myself," Burke said, "I'd like an Irish whiskey, on the rocks. And I won't assume to have the authority to speak for you ladies." It was a generous statement. She knew that Burke often made decisions for others. Very often, whether wanted, or not.

Svetlana said, making a peevish point of doing it before Tatiana, "I'll have a vodka martini, three-to-one vodka to vermouth, and garnished with three stuffed olives."

She and Tatiana exchanged a look. There was no rancor in it, and Svetlana felt rather guilty for her own unattractive behavior, even if she had pretty much kept the emotion to herself. She promised herself she'd make amends soon.

"I'll have the same," Tatiana said. She smiled at Svetlana. "It sounds delicious."

The waitress looked at Tatiana, then at Burke and, after several seconds of silence, said, "But . . ."

Burke shot the bar manager a cold-eyed look. The manager reacted immediately.

"Make sure their drinks are all on the house," he told the waitress.

"That won't be necessary. I'll be buying," Burke said.

In a soft voice, the waitress said, "I'm sorry. My mistake. Please forgive."

"Nothing to forgive." Burke's tone was the very essence of kindness. "You've been nothing less than delightful."

There are about fifty good reasons to love that man, and he's just shown one of them.

Flittering across the surface of her mind came a myriad of possibilities on just exactly how she might prove to him that she loved him, but Svetlana tried to push them more toward the back of her consciousness. When she was with Burke, thoughts of being on her knees or on her back were always only just seconds away.

But there was also Tatiana to think about, since she was sitting close enough to her left that Svetlana could feel her thighs against her own. Then Svetlana remembered that in the past she had felt more than just Tatiana's thigh touching her.

Stop thinking that way.

Silence descended upon the trio until the drinks came, and when the waitress served then exited, Burke lifted his drink and said, "To a successful and safe mission."

They clinked glasses. Svetlana took a sip of her drink, then a second. She wanted a certain level of fortification, since she wasn't at all confident of what was going on now, or what would happen in the future.

After making certain that they were in a place in the saloon where no one could hear them, Burke cleared his throat, then leaned toward the table, closer to the women. Svetlana understood the body posture. What he was about to say was important to national security, and Svetlana needed to pay careful attention to every word.

"We've got a situation where some politicians in high places are selling our government's secrets to a country that most definitely is an enemy. The politicians are guilty as hell, but we can't say anything about it because if we do, then we let our enemies know how we got the information, and the first thing they'll do is change all their operational plans. If that happens, we'll be at Ground Zero, like we were from the very beginning."

"So, we've got to stop them, but do it in such a manner that the bad guys won't know how it is that we know what they know?" Svetlana asked. She felt her palms get clammy. This was a new kind of mission for her.

"This means that it can't be an executive action," Burke said, then made a disdainful face briefly.

Executive action? Ha. Such a nice euphemism for assassination.

There were times when she wished—most times, actually—that the people she worked for, and the government she worked for, would simply come right out and say what they actually mean. Executive action? When an executive in a Fortune 500 company makes a decision, that's an executive action. When someone at Omega Force decides that an enemy of the state must be killed, that's an assassination.

She loathed the fact that some people were making a CEO's executive's decision the same as a death sentence.

Well, at least for once they're not asking me to kill anyone.

Svetlana began to think that this mission might not be so bad after all . . . even if she did have a partner.

"These men have got to be destroyed politically, and as quickly as possible," Burke said, then took a sip of his drink.

Svetlana watched as the muscles in his shoulders tightened, and then relaxed. He was becoming comfortable in discussing the assignment, she realized, and she wondered whether he would invite her up to his hotel room later. It was something she always looked forward to with unalloyed anticipation. Beneath the table, she crossed her legs at the knee, and felt a soft but gentle tingling begin in her clitoris. This meeting was getting better by the second.

"They're selling our most sensitive secrets regarding surface to air defenses, and where and how our submarines are being deployed, and how we're keeping them hidden."

Tatiana said, "But two are two entirely different segments of our military."

Svetlana was surprised but pleased that Tatiana had immediately realized that.

"The politicians are in two separate committees, one of the House of Representatives, the other in the Senate. They were both approached by the same government." Burke closed his eyes for the briefest moment. "We're bleeding top secret information, and every day that goes by, we bleed a little more." He groaned as though in physical pain. "They're in the highest level, most senior positions in two critical committees. They've got access to everything, and they're selling everything they get their hands on."

Svetlana said, "So we've got to take them down without killing them, and whatever we do it's got to seem as though we didn't know they were bent. If we do, the bad guys will reverse engineer what we've done, and shut the system down. If that happens, we'll have won the battle but lost the war."

"Exactly," Burke said. "Since there's two of them, and this takedown has to happen as quickly as possible, you're both assigned." He closed his eyes once again, took a sip of his cocktail, then looked directly into Tatiana's eyes. "However, inquiries have been made recently. We've put together a pretty good background cover for you, but there are certain bad actors in the world who are questioning it. Before I'm comfortable sending you out on another assignment, we've got to figure out some way of making the false background Omega Force has written for you seem so legitimate that only a paranoid fool would question it."

Svetlana asked, "How's my cover?"

She felt marrow-deep relief when Burke look at her and replied, "As solid as granite. After all these years, it's not doubted. It's not even question."

It hasn't been all that many years.

She wanted to tell him that, but didn't. But it had been years operating undercover, and that meant she'd been under constant, unending psychological pressure. She couldn't pretend otherwise.

Without entirely thinking through what she was about to say, Svetlana looked at Burke, placed her hand on the warm, velvety thigh of Tatiana, midway between her knee and hip, and said, "I know just how we're going to solidify Tatiana's cover story so that it's never questioned again."

ABOUT THE AUTHOR

Robin Gideon is the author of over 50 novels and novellas in paperback form and for e-publishers. She is currently writing erotic action-adventure stories starring the secret agent Svetlana Simonov exclusively for eXtasy Books. She was the featured author on the nationally syndicated TV series CBS Sunday Morning. She loves hearing from her readers, and can be reached at: robin.gideon@ymail.com.